Like Mitch, Perrie tried to hold herself apart.

Then, with a broken sob, she surrendered. She leaned into his chest, her hands gripping his shirt.

It felt like heaven. Like home. Like everything Mitch had ever wanted. And everything he would never have.

"Perrie," he groaned.

She lifted her head from his shoulder, her face only a breath from his own.

Within her, he saw an answering need. A need for refuge, for sanctuary from the cold and darkness. A loneliness that just might match his own.

His conscious mind knew this was a bad idea. But his damnable heart didn't care.

He'd been alone for so long. For just one moment, he wanted to warm himself at her and her little son's sweet fire.

Just one moment—was it so much to ask?

Dear Reader,

It's going to be a wonderful year! After all, we're celebrating Silhouette's 20th anniversary of bringing you compelling, emotional, contemporary romances month after month.

January's fabulous lineup starts with beloved author Diana Palmer, who returns to Special Edition with *Matt Caldwell: Texas Tycoon*. In the latest installment of her wildly popular LONG, TALL TEXANS series, temperatures rise and the stakes are high when a rugged tycoon meets his match in an innocent beauty—who is also his feisty employee.

Bestselling author Susan Mallery continues the next round of the series PRESCRIPTION: MARRIAGE with *Their Little Princess*. In this heart-tugging story, baby doctor Kelly Hall gives a suddenly single dad lessons in parenting—and learns all about romance!

Reader favorite Pamela Toth launches Special Edition's newest series, SO MANY BABIES—in which babies and romance abound in the Buttonwood Baby Clinic. In *The Baby Legacy*, a sperm-bank mix-up brings two unlikely parents together temporarily—or perhaps forever....

In Peggy Webb's passionate story, *Summer Hawk*, two Native Americans put aside their differences when they unite to battle a medical crisis and find that love cures all. Rounding off the month is veteran author Pat Warren's poignant, must-read secret baby story, *Daddy by Surprise*, and Jean Brashear's *Lonesome No More*, in which a reclusive hero finds healing for his heart when he offers a single mom and her young son a haven from harm.

I hope you enjoy these six unforgettable romances and help us celebrate Silhouette's 20th anniversary all year long!

Best,

Karen Taylor Richman
Senior Editor

Please address questions and book requests to:
Silhouette Reader Service
U.S.: 3010 Walden Have., P.O. Box 1325, Buffalo, NY 14269
Canadian: P.O. Box 609, Fort Erie, Ont. L2A 5X3

JEAN BRASHEAR
LONESOME NO MORE

Published by Silhouette Books
America's Publisher of Contemporary Romance

To Seneca of the timeless soul, the generous heart, the inner
beauty that exceeds even her lovely appearance; To Jonny of
the romantic bent, the fertile imagination and the independent
streak a mile wide. Thank you for making my life sparkle, for
surviving my mistakes and for honoring me with your love.
And to wonderful Matt, a warm and heartfelt welcome.

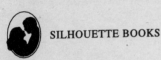 SILHOUETTE BOOKS

ISBN 0-373-24302-2

LONESOME NO MORE

Copyright © 2000 by Jean Brashear

This edition published by arrangement with Harlequin Books S.A.

Visit us at www.romance.net

Printed in U.S.A.

Books by Jean Brashear

Silhouette Special Edition

The Bodyguard's Bride #1206
A Family Secret #1266
Lonesome No More #1302

JEAN BRASHEAR

A fifth-generation Texan with pioneer roots, Jean Brashear hopes her forebears would be proud of her own leap into a new world. A lifelong avid reader, she decided when her last child was leaving the nest to try writing a book. The venture has led her in directions she never dreamed. She would tell you that she's had her heart in her throat more than once—but she's never felt more alive.

Her leap was rewarded when she sold her first novel, and Jean is hard at work on future releases while pinching herself to be sure that she isn't dreaming all this. Happily married to her own hero, and the proud mother of two fascinating children, Jean is grateful for the chance to share through her stories her heartfelt belief that love has the power to change the world.

Jean loves to hear from readers. Send a SASE for reply to P.O. Box 40012, Georgetown, TX 78628 or find her on the internet via the Harlequin/Silhouette web site at http://www.romance.net.

IT'S OUR 20th ANNIVERSARY!
We'll be celebrating all year, starting with these fabulous titles, on sale in January 2000.

Special Edition

#1297 Matt Caldwell: Texas Tycoon
Diana Palmer

#1298 Their Little Princess
Susan Mallery

#1299 The Baby Legacy
Pamela Toth

#1300 Summer Hawk
Peggy Webb

#1301 Daddy by Surprise
Pat Warren

#1302 Lonesome No More
Jean Brashear

Intimate Moments

#979 Murdock's Last Stand
Beverly Barton

#980 Marrying Mike... Again
Alicia Scott

#981 A Drive-By Wedding
Terese Ramin

#982 Midnight Promises
Eileen Wilks

#983 The Comeback of Con MacNeill
Virginia Kantra

#984 Witness... and Wife?
Kate Stevenson

Romance

#1420 The Baby Bequest
Susan Meier

#1421 With a Little T.L.C.
Teresa Southwick

#1422 The Sheik's Solution
Barbara McMahon

#1423 Annie and the Prince
Elizabeth Harbison

#1424 A Babe in the Woods
Cara Colter

#1425 Prim, Proper... Pregnant
Alice Sharpe

Desire

#1267 Her Forever Man
Leanne Banks

#1268 The Pregnant Princess
Anne Marie Winston

#1269 Dr. Mommy
Elizabeth Bevarly

#1270 Hard Lovin' Man
Peggy Moreland

#1271 The Cowboy Takes a Bride
Cathleen Galitz

#1272 Skyler Hawk: Lone Brave
Sheri WhiteFeather

Chapter One

Wind River Range, Wyoming

A broken cry drifted on the wind, slicing into the silence that was his trusted companion.

Inside the cabin, Mitch Gallagher's hands stilled on the tent he was mending. He frowned and turned his head slightly, listening.

Nothing.

No—wait. There it was again, choppy but getting stronger. No animal he'd ever heard sounded like that. It almost sounded like a child, but camping season was over, and no children lived within miles of this very isolated cabin.

He dropped the tent and touched the scabbard at

his waist. The knife he'd always carried had been replaced by the one Cy had left him. He missed the old man still.

Just then he heard footsteps, too light to be adult. Broken sobs hit a counterpoint, then a thin, high wail.

Mitch had the front door open in seconds.

"Help, mister—my mom's hurt."

For one single instant, a sharp pain sliced through his heart. The boy looked just like—

No. Of course it wasn't Boone. His brother wasn't a child anymore, hadn't been in years.

But Mitch's hands still trembled slightly on the doorknob. He descended from the porch of the cabin in quick strides. "What happened? Where's your mother? Are you alone?"

The boy's eyes went wide at the sound of his voice, and he backed away slightly. Mitch realized he must seem huge to someone so small, so he dropped to one knee on the ground in front of the boy and gentled his voice. "Are you all right?"

The boy's cheeks were scratched, his shirt torn at the shoulder. Still frozen in place, his face white and bloodless, the boy breathed in harsh, sharp gasps.

Mitch reached out and clasped the child's shoulders. A shudder ran through the boy, then his teeth began to chatter.

"Son, are you hurt? Tell me where your mother is so I can help her."

No response, just the raspy sobs of a child approaching hysteria.

Mitch felt the child's limbs and ran his hands over the boy's hair, finding nothing but scratches and bruises beginning to form. But the boy continued to stare at him.

"Hey, it's all right—" Mitch pulled the boy close, intending to comfort him.

The motion galvanized the child into action. "No—don't hurt me—"

Mitch's hands dropped away instantly. "All right. Calm down. Take a deep breath. Tell me where your mother is."

The little body visibly trembled, but the boy straightened and looked around him like he'd never seen the place before. His eyes filled with tears again. "I—I don't know."

"Son, look at me." Mitch kept his voice pitched softly, like he would with a wounded animal.

The boy watched him with suspicion too old for his years.

"We're going to find your mother. Don't worry. I can track anything that moves, but it's going to be dark soon. I could use your help."

"Me?" The blue eyes widened. "I'm just a little kid."

"Not too little to help me look. Now tell me which direction you came from."

"Over there." The boy pointed. "My grandpa's cabin was supposed to be this way." His lower lip quivered. "My mom said it wasn't far, right before she fell down." Tears filled his eyes again. "She won't talk to me. Is she dead?" He rushed on without an answer, his words tumbling over one another. "Where's Grandpa Cy? He was gonna help us."

Grandpa *Cy?* Dear God, it couldn't be—Mitch clasped the boy's shoulders. "What's your mom's name, son?" Surely she wouldn't—Mitch almost missed the name in the confusion of his thoughts.

"What?"

"Perrie. Perrie Matheson, that's my mom's name."

It *was* her—Cy's granddaughter from Boston. The callous socialite who had broken his only friend's heart. Who hadn't cared enough to call or write, wouldn't even take Mitch's call when he'd left Cy's side for the three-hour trip to a phone, scared to his bones that Cy would die while he was gone. He'd been prepared to beg, and she'd been too busy to answer a damn phone. Mitch rose to pace.

"What's wrong, mister?"

Mitch shot the boy a quick frown and saw him take a step back. Looking down, Mitch saw that his hands were clenched into fists. He was probably scaring the kid to death. He sucked in a deep breath and forced himself to remain calm. Emotions were useless. Nothing good came of feeling too much. And sometimes you lost more than you could bear.

The kid wasn't at fault for his mother's sins. And

Mitch had promised. He didn't renege on a promise. For the boy, not for her, he would do this.

"Okay. Stay behind me and stay quiet unless you see something familiar. Don't get in front of me, whatever you do, because you'll obscure the tracks I'm looking for. Got it?"

"Yes, sir." The boy ducked his head, and Mitch could still see tears sparkle on his lashes.

Like he was about to touch a coiled rattler, Mitch reached out one hand and laid it on the boy's head, surprised by the softness of the golden hair. He drew his hand back as if burned.

"We'll find her, son."

"Yes, sir." And like a little soldier, the boy drew himself up straight. "I'll be quiet." He looked ahead to the way he'd pointed, and Mitch could almost see the resolve of the man the boy would become.

How had a pampered, selfish woman produced this child?

It didn't matter. She was probably fine, just didn't have the stamina to make the two-mile hike up the mountain. Instead, she'd sent this poor little guy for help. Mitch would find her, tell her what he thought of her and send them on their way. Cy had given Mitch this cabin after he'd given up on his granddaughter caring whether he lived or died. Though home was a luxury Mitch never expected to know again, he would be damned if that woman would spend a single hour inside the only place that had welcomed him in the last sixteen years.

"Come on, son. Let's get a move on."

It didn't take long to spot the figure lying beneath a tree. They'd gotten pretty close to the cabin. Still, a quarter of a mile through a dark, unfamiliar forest had to be scary for someone so small.

"Mom!" The boy ran past him, dropping down beside her.

Mitch followed, hoping for the kid's sake that she was only sleeping. Then he came near enough to get a good look.

Like Sleeping Beauty, she lay there as if under a spell. Wisps of golden hair escaped from a long braid that would extend almost to her waist. He knelt beside her and felt for a pulse, the boy's eyes following his every move.

"Is she dead?"

Strong and steady. "No. She's not dead." He felt her forehead and quickly pulled his fingers away. Damn. She was burning up with fever. A quick, impersonal scan told him nothing seemed to be broken.

He looked at the boy. "Did she say she was feeling bad?"

"She said her throat hurt, so she couldn't talk to me much. She had to stop a lot after we left the car."

The cabin lay two miles inside a designated wilderness area, on one of the few private tracts enclosed by government land. All motorized objects were prohibited—even bicycles were not allowed.

There were no phones and no electric lines. The mountains were so rugged that cell phones weren't reliable and two-way radios required a repeater, which only the ranger station had. The isolation had suited Cy just fine, and Mitch, as well. But right now he cursed the lack of resources. He could carry her two miles to his truck, but he doubted the boy could walk that far again, and carrying both would be tricky. The nearest medical facility was eight hours away.

Mitch swore silently. She looked exhausted and painfully thin. The boy looked better, but his own exhaustion was showing.

Sore throat and fever—maybe it was just the flu. If she were anyone else, it would make sense to take her to the cabin and check her temperature before taking any more radical action.

But she wasn't anyone else. She was callous and uncaring and had let Cy die alone except for a man who was no blood relation.

Mitch looked at the boy, saw his fear and fatigue. Then he looked back at the woman.

Even now she was beautiful. Delicate, so small she looked like a child herself, her figure hidden beneath layers of clothing. A backpack cut into her shoulders, its bulk twisting her body to one side. Another one, smaller and brightly colored, lay beside her. He reached out to remove the big one, surprised at its heft.

"You won't hurt her, will you?" Like a tiny warrior, the boy moved closer to his mother.

Mitch frowned, but shook his head. Despite what she'd done to Cy, he would never hurt her. "She's got a fever. When's the last time she drank anything?"

"This morning, I think."

"Did you carry any water?"

"Just my lunchbox thermos."

"Your mom carry any?"

He shook his head. "Her water bottle fell and broke, but she said she would drink some when we got to Grandpa Cy's cabin. Do you know my grandpa Cy?"

Mitch was too angry to discuss Cy right now. What was she thinking of, putting the boy in a vulnerable position like this? Couldn't she tell she was sick? What if Mitch had been out guiding, as was normal this time of year? She and the boy could have died out here.

He made up his mind. The boy needed rest and food. "Come on, son. Let's get you back to the cabin."

He picked her up easily, draping the backpack over his shoulder. "Can you carry that one or do you need me to do it?"

The boy lifted the bright green-and-yellow pack and squared his shoulders again. "I can do it. Just make my mom better, please, mister."

For a woman who had shown little evidence of either character or heart, this little guy had enough for both of them. Feeling an odd tightness in his throat, Mitch merely nodded and led the way.

* * *

Mitch laid her down on the bed in Cy's room. So tiny. So fragile. So pale.

"You sure she's not dead?"

Mitch frowned and turned, seeing the boy struggle, his blue eyes swimming with tears.

"Yes." What did you do with a little kid? "She's just passed out."

"Is she gonna die?" The boy's lower lip quivered, but he stood straight and studied Mitch.

A long-buried arrowhead surfaced. Mitch knew what it was like to watch a mother die. "No," he grated. "She won't die."

The boy moved a step closer to his mother, standing between her and Mitch. "Can you make her well?"

What are you doing here? Mitch wanted to ask. *Go away. Leave me alone. Your mother let your grandfather die unwanted.*

But he was just a kid. Even if she was heartless, she was still his mother.

"I think so. Listen—" He dropped to his heels. "What's your name?"

The boy hesitated. "I'm not supposed to talk to strangers. Especially men."

A little late for that, but Mitch nodded seriously. "That's good advice. But since your grandpa Cy was my best friend, I guess that makes us not so much strangers."

The boy pondered the statement. He nodded but still didn't answer.

Mitch held out his hand. "My name is Mitch."

The boy darted a glance to his mother's still form and then back. Finally he placed his much-smaller hand in Mitch's. "My name is Davey." Then, as if remembering a lesson in manners, he added, "Pleased to meet you."

Mitch stifled a grin and shook the boy's hand. "All right, Davey. First thing we have to do is take care of your mom's fever." He rose to his feet. "You can help me."

"Me?" Blue eyes goggled.

"Yeah, you. Unless you're too little."

"I'm not too little." Davey's chest puffed out from his sturdy little body. "I can help."

Mitch nodded. "Good. You stay right here so she'll see you if she wakes up. I'm going to get a thermometer from my first-aid pack."

When he returned, the boy was watching his mother as if she might vanish if he didn't. *She's not worth it, kid,* he wanted to say. But Mitch said nothing; he merely opened her mouth and put the thermometer under her tongue, then sat on the edge of the mattress and carefully held her slack jaw shut, glancing at his watch to time himself.

"You ever run a fever?"

Tousled blond hair bounced as the boy nodded.

"What did she do?"

His brow wrinkled. "She stuck a thermometer in my ear."

"Your ear?" What kind of mother was she? "Why not under your tongue?" Mitch could still recall having to hold one for what seemed forever, waiting for his mother to get a reading.

"That's the old way Mom told me."

Mitch shook his head. Must be some new kind of thermometer. "What else did she do?"

"She stuck me in a bathtub full of water once." He smiled. "It felt so cold I screamed."

Mitch had to smile back. "I'll bet."

Davey moved closer to his mother. "Mom," he whispered earnestly, "wake up." In his voice, Mitch heard the cracking edge of desperation, but Davey stood between her and Mitch as if to guard her. Something about the boy's fierceness touched Mitch.

Not all mothers were angels, but he couldn't tell such a little kid that his mother was a jerk. Worse than a jerk. She'd married some fat cat and turned her back on a damn fine man.

A man who'd saved his life. If not for Cyrus Blackburn, Mitch Gallagher would be in jail—or dead. Cy had seen past the angry young man to the boy who had lost everything. Who'd been banished, accused and convicted without a trial. He'd had to watch his mother's funeral from a distance and then leave Morning Star, Texas, forever.

He'd learned not to feel. Not to need. But he owed Cy more than he could ever repay, and this woman had hurt Cy. Refused contact when the old man needed her most.

The woman stirred and moaned. Mitch edged

closer to her, making sure the thermometer stayed put for another fifteen seconds.

"I wish I could find Grandpa Cy," the boy whispered. "Mom said he could do anything. He'd make Mom wake up, I bet."

Unwelcome tightness crowded Mitch's throat. Should he tell the boy? It wasn't fair to leave him hoping, but what did you say to a little kid at a time like this?

"Listen, Davey—" Mitch swore silently, wishing he were anywhere but here. Anyone would be better than him at doing this. He wasn't a man with pretty words.

Davey just watched him solemnly, those big blue eyes looking so vulnerable. The kid had been stronger than he had any right to expect.

Mitch would just have to keep him busy until his mother woke up. Then it was her job to figure out how to tell him. "Let's just concentrate on getting your mother well right now."

The little voice sank low, almost to a whisper. "I don't know how." He looked away, like the failure was his.

What did Mitch know about dealing with kids? "How old are you?"

Blue eyes swam with despair. "Five."

Five years old. Mitch tried to remember being five. All he could recall was the first day his own grandpa Ben had helped a kid with clumsy fingers learn to bait a hook.

And how it felt to succeed.

Okay. They'd start small. "Well, first you take hold of the thermometer and hand it to me."

"What if I break it?"

"I don't think you will. Do you?"

The boy shot a sideways glance at the thin glass tube, then shook his head. "No, sir."

"Then hand it to me and let's see if we need to dunk your mom in a tub."

Through the boy's fear, a tiny smile peeked out. He handled the thermometer as if it were the finest china, then gave it to Mitch.

Mitch eyeballed the reading. One hundred and two. Keeping his face carefully neutral, he looked back at Davey. He wouldn't scare the boy, but he wouldn't coddle him, either. "It's pretty high, son, but nothing we can't handle. You watch her and call out if she wakes up. I'm headed to get water."

"You're really going to stick her in a tub of cold water?"

Mitch almost smiled at the boy's horror. "No, but I need to sponge her down."

Davey looked dubious. "What if she screams?"

Mitch glanced back on his way out the door. "At least she'll be awake."

"Yes, sir." To the boy's credit, there was only a tiny tremble in his voice. He stood like a little sentinel, guarding his mother.

Mitch shook his head and turned away, wondering if Davey's mother knew that she didn't deserve him.

* * *

The flames licked at her face. Around her, they rose to taunt her. On the other side of the fire, Simon clutched a struggling Davey. "I told you not to involve the police. You're a fool to defy me, Perrie. Mathesons always win."

Not this time. Oh please, not this time.

Hot. So hot. She was going to die and he would hurt Davey.

"No—" she screamed, but no sound erupted from her blistered throat. Desperately she summoned the strength to lift feet gone leaden, hands turned to stone—

"Davey—"

But he was gone. Vanished. She knew she would never see him again. He was her heart. He was everything—

"Shh," a deep rumble murmured. "Easy. Lie still."

Cool. The blessing of moisture slid over her skin. A strong arm slid beneath her back and lifted her.

"Grandpa?" Perrie opened her eyes.

Golden brown eyes turned to stone. A strong jaw flexed. "Drink this," ordered a man she'd never seen before.

"Who—" Her throat hurt so badly. She stiffened and tried to scramble away, but her limbs wouldn't move. "Who are you? Davey—where is he? Where's my son?"

"He's asleep. Drink this."

"I don't believe you. I have to see—"

The big body shifted. Past his broad shoulders,

she saw a familiar blond head lying on a cot beside the wall. Her son was the picture of peace, snoring faintly. She gathered herself to go to him, but her body wouldn't obey her.

"Take it easy. He's just asleep. Nothing's wrong."

Head spinning, she closed her eyes and fought the tears, her fingers tightening on an arm that felt like granite.

She shifted her gaze back to the man who held her. Across a rugged, handsome face framed by shaggy dark hair, distrust and dislike warred with a tiny flicker of sympathy.

"He stayed awake a long time to protect you, but he finally went out like a light."

"How long have I been asleep? What time is it?"

"A little after two. Now drink this." Any sympathy had vanished.

"What is it?"

"Same thing I've forced down your throat for hours. Aspirin crushed in water. You've got a hell of a fever."

It hurt to swallow, but she downed the whole thing, then lay back, exhausted. She peered around the room that was lit by a single kerosene lantern.

Her breath caught. She knew this room.

Her gaze flew to his. "Who are you? What have you done with my grandfather?"

He didn't hide his contempt. "What do you care?

Why did you come now? Here to pick the carcass clean?''

She squeezed her eyes shut. This had to be a nightmare. But when she opened them, the same hard eyes met hers. ''What are you talking about?''

''Don't play innocent. You didn't care enough to call or write, much less come see an old man who loved you, not even when he was dying. Don't expect a welcome mat now.''

''He's—'' Perrie couldn't make herself say the words. For more than two thousand miles, her only thought had been that her grandfather would help her save her son from Simon, the monster who was Davey's father.

''Cy is dead,'' the stranger grated. ''And I want you out of this cabin the second you're able. There's no place for you here.'' His rock-hard jaw flexed, those eyes boring into her as though he could turn her to stone.

She couldn't even cry, so deep was the despair she felt. ''How did he—''

His eyes flashed as though he couldn't bear the very sight of her.

She fell silent, too dizzy and weary, every bone in her body aching. But she had to ask one last thing. ''Davey—please. Please don't hurt him. I'll take care of him—'' She struggled with the covers, thinking she must get to her son, protect him from this man who hated her for some reason she couldn't understand. But she couldn't seem to untangle herself. Her muscles had turned to water.

"The boy is fine." Hard brown eyes turned curiously gentle for one brief second. "He's a great kid. I won't let anything happen to him." Then his gaze focused on her again, and the gentleness vanished. "Go back to sleep." He dismissed her curtly and headed for the door.

Perrie wanted to explain. Wanted to understand. Wanted out of here, away from that man.

Then the dream flickered, and she remembered.

She had nowhere else to go.

Davey was all that mattered. The silent man had tucked him into a cot and set his shoes neatly beneath it. Her son's face bore a look of innocent trust, not fear. But how could she trust a total stranger?

She couldn't think, couldn't scrape away the mist that fogged her mind, pinning her helplessly to the bed.

Grandpa was dead. Her ex-husband had threatened to take Davey away to where she would never find him if she breathed a word about Simon's crimes.

And a tall, forbidding stranger wanted her out of the refuge she'd dreamed of during all the years of Simon's prison.

Perrie fought to stay awake, to remain alert for any sound her son might make. Tomorrow. Tomorrow she would figure out the answers.

But even as she fought, sleep crept into her muzzy thoughts on silent cat feet…and claimed her.

* * *

"Mister." The whisper tickled his ear.

Mitch opened his eyes to see frantic blue ones.

"I can't find the bathroom." Davey was bouncing on his toes, holding himself.

"Uh—" Mitch groaned and sat up. "Go out on the porch."

"What?" Blue eyes goggled. "The bathroom's on the porch?" He was shifting from one foot to the other.

"You ever pee outside?"

If Mitch weren't feeling the effects of the night's frequent interruptions, he'd laugh at the kid's expression. Levering himself up off the bed, he stood up.

"You don't got any pajamas on."

Mitch reached for his jeans and slipped them on over the briefs he didn't usually wear to bed. "Nobody invited you in my room."

"I was—I didn't know—"

Mitch quelled his irritation. Shrugging on a shirt, he sat down to pull on socks, shaking out his boots in a habit that was years old. "Go on outside."

"It's dark out there." Davey was rocking back and forth now.

Mitch jerked on his boots and sighed, picking Davey up under one arm like a sack of feed and heading for the front door. "Where are your shoes?"

"In my room."

"Watch where you're standing, and don't walk around barefoot anymore."

"Something will bite me?"

"This isn't the city, kid." He set the boy down after checking the porch for undesirables. "Okay, go ahead. I'll show you the outhouse later."

Davey looked confused. "Here?"

Mitch sighed again. "Yeah, here. Unless you want to wait to get your shoes, then head around to the back of the cabin."

"Mom wouldn't like this."

"Mom's not watching."

"Don't look."

"I'm not looking." Mitch leaned against the support post with his back turned and listened to the aspens whisper. Very quickly another sound joined the night.

"Wow, look how far I can hit."

Mitch couldn't help a smile at the boy's delight. It brought back memories of boyhood competitions with his brother. Soon the sound stopped. "You ready?"

Davey walked back to his side. "It's cold out here."

"You got any warm clothes?"

"I guess. In the car."

"We'll have to make do, then." He couldn't leave Davey alone here, with her so sick. "Come back inside."

Davey didn't move. "What if I step on something bad? I can't see where I'm going."

Mitch swooped him up and settled the boy on his back.

"Wow, you're really tall. My dad's not so tall."

"Where is your dad?"

The small body stiffened. "I don't know." The voice turned faint and confiding. "He doesn't like me."

A tiny corner of Mitch's well-guarded heart opened. *Welcome to the club, kid. My dad hates me.* "Your mom loves you. That's good enough." *Be grateful you have one.*

"Yeah, I guess so." Warm breath whistled across Mitch's ear. Sturdy little arms tightened around his neck. One foot brushed Mitch's arm. It was ice-cold.

"Let's get you back to bed."

"Mister?"

"I said you can call me Mitch."

"Okay." A pregnant pause hovered.

"What?"

"I'm hungry."

Baby-sitter…nurse…cook… What else would he have to become before he could get the woman out of his cabin? "Not sleepy?"

Soft hair brushed against his neck. "Uh-uh," the boy whispered. "Is that okay?"

Poor kid. Not his fault his mother was heartless. Or that his dad didn't care. Mitch had been alone since age sixteen, except for Cyrus Blackburn. This little guy was alone in a strange place with a strange man and a sick mother.

"Yeah." He squeezed one chilled foot in each hand. "That's okay. Let me check on your mom and then we'll fix some breakfast."

Chapter Two

Perrie braced herself against the doorjamb, trying to decide how long she'd slept. The front door seemed miles away. Unless Grandpa had added on facilities she couldn't see, she had a long walk after that.

Grandpa. A wave of grief threatened to drown her.

Not now, Perrie. You've got to find Davey. Got to figure this out. One step at a time. You can grieve later.

First to the chair hewn from logs, its handmade cushions calling like a siren. She could make it that far, surely. Perrie concentrated as though life hung in the balance. When she touched the back, she clung to keep from collapsing.

Where was Davey? Had the hard-eyed stranger grown tired of him and left? Davey knew nothing about the forest, nothing about mountains. He could fall, there were bears, he could be—

The front door opened with a gust of cool air. Davey raced inside, vibrating with excitement.

"Keep it quiet. Your mom—" The golden-eyed stranger broke off in midsentence.

Davey looked up from the bucket of freshly cleaned fish he was holding. "Mom—" He dropped the bucket and came running, plastering himself to her side.

Perrie gripped him hard, stroking his hair and trying not to sink to the floor. Then she looked back at the man who filled the doorframe like some mythical figure. Dark hair teased the collar of his red plaid flannel shirt. His face was all hard planes and dark hollows. What little light had been in his eyes when he'd been looking at her son, vanished into stone when he looked at her.

"What are you doing out of bed?"

"I just need to—" She glanced toward the outside. The lack of amenities had been no big deal when she'd been a kid here with her grandfather. Explaining to a strange man was another matter.

He frowned, then understanding dawned. "Davey," he ordered. "Go get your mom's shoes and bring them here."

"Okay, Mitch." Davey obeyed instantly.

The man named Mitch set the fishing rod and

tackle box by the door and crossed to her. Without a word, he scooped her up into his arms.

"I don't need—"

"You're about to pass out and you know it." Over his shoulder he spoke to her son. "Slip them on her feet. That's right. Now stay here for a few minutes. I'm taking your mom around back."

"Can't she just go off the porch, too, Mitch?"

For a second so brief she could have imagined it, Perrie thought she saw laughter in the amber eyes. If only she weren't so dizzy—

"No. Girls can't go off the porch. Stay right here until we get back. You can help me cook the fish."

"Okay!"

Relieved to hear only enthusiasm in her son's voice, Perrie's anxiety eased a little. The man seemed good to Davey—firm but kind. She wished she knew how to thank him. She wished she weren't so shaky.

She wished she knew why he hated her.

Then they were through the door and headed around the cabin toward the outhouse.

Perrie tried to summon the strength to be embarrassed, but somehow he made it all matter-of-fact, setting her down and walking away until she emerged again. Then he scooped her back into his arms and headed around the cabin.

"Thank you," she murmured, trying not to lean against his broad chest. It was a cruel taunt that she felt so safe in his arms. As her eyes drifted closed, against her cheek she felt hard muscle play beneath

warm flannel. He smelled of forest and sunshine—
and strong, healthy male. For a moment Perrie wondered what it would be like to relax in this man's
care.

It didn't matter. He despised her. Somehow she
had to find the strength to take charge, to make new
plans.

They'd come so far, only to find everything lost.
For so long her only thought had been to make it
to this place of safety, where Grandpa could help
her figure out how to fight off Simon and his powerful family.

Maybe it had only been a nightmare. Perrie lifted
a head that felt like it weighed ten tons. "I didn't
dream it? Grandpa Cy is really dead?"

The granite jaw tightened more. "What do you
care?"

Perrie forgot about safety and comfort. She struggled to leave the arms of a man who could believe
that she wouldn't care about losing the finest man
she'd ever known. Cyrus Blackburn had been rough
as a cob and a man from the wrong century, but
he'd had compassion and honor enough for a dozen
men.

"Be still." His arms tightened, trapping her.
"We're almost there."

"Let me down. You don't understand anything."
She wanted to explain about Simon, but she was
too ashamed that she'd been so weak. She wanted
answers from him about why he was here, about

how Grandpa had died. About why he thought she wouldn't care.

Her vision grayed as she struggled. She was so tired. So drained. *Be quiet, Perrie. You don't know if you can trust him. The only man you knew you could trust is dead.* And she'd never had a chance to say goodbye.

"I understand that there's a little boy in there who needs his mother to get well. Don't be a fool."

Perrie bit her lip hard. He was right. All that mattered was being able to take care of Davey. She would grieve in private. This man would not believe her tears, anyway.

Perrie stopped struggling. But she couldn't seem to stop the ache inside her chest.

When he carried her inside, she reached down to stroke her son's hair.

"Are you better, Mom? Can you stay in here with us? We'll cook you some fish. I caught one of them. Mitch showed me how."

Perrie tried to reassure him with a smile. "Sweetie, I—"

Before she could steady her voice, Mitch spoke up. "Your mom needs more sleep so she can get well. Maybe tomorrow."

She was forced to be grateful for his intervention. At least he was kind to her son.

Arms stiff as though carrying an unwelcome burden, he walked back to the room that smelled of her grandfather's pipe. He laid her down, then turned away.

"He was the best man I ever knew," she whispered.

"Too bad you broke his heart." With long strides he left the room, closing the door behind him.

Perrie curled up in a ball and buried her face in the pillow so no one would hear her cry.

Davey stood on a chair beside him, tracing designs in the cornmeal with his fish. "Mitch?"

Mitch watched the grease, waiting for the bubbles to signal that it was ready. "Yeah?"

"Why don't you like my mom?"

Mitch glanced over to see the boy's brow furrowed, his blue eyes dark and sad. The kid was too smart. How did you tell a child about betrayal? "What makes you think I don't like her?"

Davey shrugged. "Your voice just gets sorta mean when you talk to her."

Mitch exhaled in a gust. "I don't know your mom. She's been sick ever since she got here."

"I can take care of her if it makes you mad."

Oh, hell. "It doesn't make me mad." Not exactly. If only she weren't such a contrast—so damn beautiful…and such a cold heart. And if only her lying there so still and pale didn't make him remember another fragile blonde who had died in his arms—

"I miss my room and my toys. I want to go home." Davey dropped the fish. His bottom lip quivered.

Aw, man. He didn't know anything about kids. Awkwardly Mitch reached out and patted the boy's shoulder.

Davey latched on with both arms around Mitch's neck, his breath coming in short gasps and snuffles. "I don't like this place. I want my mom to get better and take me home."

Deep within Mitch memories stirred. All alone on a dark highway, everything familiar lost. Deep, wracking guilt mingled with rage and bitter knowledge that he could never go home. Nowhere to go, no one to care. He'd been sixteen and had wanted to cry himself. But he'd known somehow that if he ever started, he'd never stop. So instead he'd started fights and gotten drunk.

Poor kid. Mitch pulled Davey up off the chair and wrapped his arms tight around the small body. Davey's legs wrapped around his waist and he cried in earnest.

Mitch's rusty, unused heart ached. But he didn't try to tell the boy platitudes. Maybe it would turn out all right; maybe not. You just had to keep going, no matter what. So Mitch simply held him.

When the boy's sobbing slowed, Mitch leaned back. "Not much I can do about getting you home right now. Looks like we're stuck together. Might as well make the best of it. You know how to play checkers?"

Davey's shoulders sagged. "No."

"Then it's time you learned. After we eat, I'll teach you. Now, you still want to fry some fish?"

Davey leaned against his chest again for a moment.

Mitch closed his eyes and stroked once across soft blond hair.

The boy drew in a shuddery breath, lifted his head and nodded.

Mitch set him back on the chair as though he was dynamite, set to blow. He turned his face away quickly. "Good." He cleared his throat. "Let's fry yours first."

After ten games of checkers and another excursion to the porch, finally Davey was asleep. Mitch grinned, looking at the tousled blond hair. He was going to have to convince the little guy that the porch was for extreme circumstances, not regular use. But it gave Davey such pleasure that it was difficult for Mitch to say no.

He was a great kid. Mitch didn't understand how a woman who could raise such a terrific child could be so thoughtless toward her grandfather in his time of need. She must have been ashamed of him in her fancy new life.

From what Davey said, his father hadn't been around much. Except for his mother, the boy spent most of his time around servants. He was full of stories about pranks he'd played on the maids and jokes the butler had taught him, but he didn't have much to say about his father.

Mitch turned, checking on Perrie one last time before he went to bed himself. For a moment he just stood there, studying her. Trying to understand her.

Was she cold to everyone but her child? Davey's stories were full of his mother; there could be no doubt that she took an active part in his life. The kid could even read some, as Mitch had discovered when he'd read to him from one of Cy's favorites, an old book called *Freckles* by Gene Stratton-Porter. Davey had picked out a surprising number of words here and there.

She lay swallowed up in the bedclothes, the blond braid spilling over one shoulder. For a moment, a memory of ivory skin seared his brain. He'd tried not to notice as he'd worked to bring down her fever, but he couldn't forget the sweet curve of her hips, the tender rose of her nipples.

She was small yet perfect. A china doll who belonged on a shelf, who should be safely ensconced in a Boston mansion. Who should be wearing designer gowns and giving teas.

Instead, she was in Wyoming, in an area so remote that few men ever set foot here. She had driven far beyond the end of the road, then walked two miles with a small child through a forest she hadn't been inside for years.

And the china doll had dark smudges of exhaustion beneath her eyes and hollows in her cheeks.

Why?

Then Mitch started, realizing that her eyes were open and clear. He walked closer to the bed. ''Need anything? A drink? Or the—'' He nodded his head outside.

"Maybe some water." Perrie's throat felt like sandpaper.

He poured a drink and lifted her with one arm behind her shoulders, holding the glass to her lips.

Perrie drank long, grateful swallows. Finally she stopped and looked up at the golden eyes that had bored through her from the doorway. She glanced over at Davey.

"I'm sorry you've had to take care of him."

He stood up and shrugged, whispering, "He's a good kid."

She smiled. "You don't have to whisper. He sleeps like the dead once he's out."

The corners of his lips curved faintly. "That's the trick—getting him there."

Her smile widened. "How many stories?"

"It wasn't the stories so much. It was the ten games of checkers." His eyes sparked with wry amusement.

Perrie wondered if he knew how even a faint smile transformed his face. Power always surrounded him—a magnetism that shimmered even in his harshest moments—but that smile stole her breath.

Then the smile winked out like the Cheshire Cat. "Why?"

Perrie couldn't keep up. "Why what?"

"Why are you dragging him around the countryside? He wants to go home."

Perrie glanced away. "We came to see my grandfather."

"Your grandfather has been dead for six months."

But I didn't know that. A fresh wave of grief threatened to drown her. "Does Davey know?"

He shook his head. "I didn't think it was my place to tell him."

Perrie couldn't think about how hard it would be, telling her son that their last hope was gone. She dug her fingers into the bedspread. First things first. She needed a place to hide Davey. "Did he leave a will?"

Mitch looked at her like she had crawled out from under a rock. His voice chilled. "If you'd bothered to care, you'd know that Cy wasn't much for paperwork."

He was wrong about her, but she wouldn't argue. She couldn't let his contempt matter. Only Davey mattered. "I'm his only relative."

"Who hasn't given him a thought in years."

He had loved her grandfather. She could hear the grief in his voice.

"How did you know my grandfather?"

His jaw set, rock-hard. "He gave me a chance when no one else cared."

She wondered about the story behind his few words, but it couldn't be her concern now. Only survival was important. Only Davey's safety. She didn't know this man. Couldn't afford to trust him. "How soon will you be leaving?"

His eyes went wide, then narrowed. "Lady—" Then he glanced around to be sure Davey was still sleeping. "I'm not the one who has to leave. Cy gave me this cabin and everything he had left, once he realized you weren't coming."

"But I—" *Didn't know.*

Guilt battered at her heart. When she'd gotten her own place after the divorce, so much had been going on. She had intended to write her grandfather and give him her new address, even though he was not a man to write letters.

She would have done it, too, because she'd missed him for all those years. But then Simon had shown up again with his threats and his demands.

It was on the tip of her tongue to explain. Mitch was a hard man, a strong man who could help her.

But he couldn't wait for her to leave. And she had no choice but to stay until she could figure out what else to do. If this cabin belonged to him, she had to buy some time. It rankled her to be so helpless.

"I know I've been a lot of trouble. I'm not staying in bed tomorrow. I'll be up and pulling my weight."

"You'll be lucky if you can walk across the room." He exhaled in a gust, hands on hips. "You don't have to push it. Stay until you're strong enough." He turned and left.

Perrie closed her eyes in thanksgiving.

A reprieve. Time to plan.

* * *

Perrie made it to the table before her legs turned to spaghetti. It was barely light, and Davey still slept soundly.

Outside, she heard a steady rhythm. Glancing out the window, she saw him.

What a beautiful male animal.

Gilded by shafts of light streaking down through the trees, he could have stepped out of a legend. Stripped down to a sweat-soaked T-shirt, every muscle showed clearly the raw power of the man.

Perrie had borne a child, but she had never known desire. Simon had taken a child-woman and taught her all about sex, but nothing about passion. It had been the happiest day of her life when he had stopped visiting her bed and had gone back to his other women. When he had fallen hard enough for one of them and demanded a divorce, she had gladly agreed to any terms to escape him.

Perrie had always believed that she lacked something essential, some ability to be fully a woman. She had buried herself in being a mother and planned to live out her life alone.

But watching this man's hard, dangerous beauty, Perrie wondered.

"Mom?" From behind her, Davey's sleepy voice interrupted her thoughts. "Are you all better?"

She arose and clutched the chair as the room tilted. Quickly she sat back down. "Maybe not all better, honey, but I'm really tired of that bed."

He smiled and ran to her, wrapping his arms tightly around her neck. "I missed you, Mom." His voice dropped to a fierce whisper. "I was scared. You were sick and I don't know where Grandpa Cy is. You said he would keep us safe."

Traitorous tears threatened. Perrie hugged him tightly, then settled him on her lap. "Listen, sweetheart…I have something—" Perrie squeezed her eyes shut. She wanted Grandpa here, too.

Then she straightened her shoulders and leaned back to look into Davey's eyes. "Sweetie, Grandpa Cy got very sick and he can't be here to help us, after all."

"When will he come back?"

She swallowed hard. "He won't be coming back, Davey. Grandpa Cy is in heaven with the angels." She watched her son's beautiful blue eyes widen.

"You mean he's dead? Like Sparky?"

The only time Davey had been allowed a pet had been the brief hiatus after the divorce. His little puppy had escaped and been run over. Davey had struggled with the concept of death.

Blue eyes glistened with sudden moisture. "You said he would be here."

"Yes—" she nodded "—and I know he would want to be with us if he could. I know he's watching over us right now. You don't have to worry."

He cocked his head as if she'd spouted nonsense. "I'm not worried. Mitch is here. He'll take care of us."

Perrie knew that her son's confidence about their welcome was misplaced, but now wasn't the time to make him feel less secure. "He hasn't—he didn't hurt you or scare you?"

Davey pulled back, honestly shocked. "Mitch?" He shook his head. "Mitch is great. He showed me how to fish and he doesn't make me take a bath and he lets me—" He stopped suddenly, covering his mouth with one hand.

She couldn't help grinning. "What?"

Blue eyes went wide, and he shook his head.

"Shall I tickle you until you tell me?"

Davey squirmed to get away, but Perrie held him close, laughing. "No bath? Better tell me what else."

He giggled and squirmed harder. "Mitch said—" His eyes danced, and he shook his head.

Perrie's fingers started moving. "Mitch said what?"

"No, Mom, you—" He squealed one loud scream, then laughed harder.

Perrie was laughing, too, but she knew she'd better stop before she dropped him. "I what, sweetie? You know you want to tell me—"

The door crashed open. Mitch charged inside, looking wild and fierce—

Perrie and Davey stopped cold, both faces still wearing traces of laughter.

Mitch's heartbeat thundered. He'd heard the scream and known a fear beyond anything he'd felt in years. There was so much the boy could have hurt himself on—

He lost it. "What the hell are you doing out of bed?"

Every trace of a smile vanished. Davey's eyes filled with tears, and Perrie ruffled like a wet hen. She set her son down and rose to face Mitch like a small warrior.

A warrior whose face had all the color of a sheet of paper.

"I'm a grown woman. Don't try to tell me—"

"Sit down before you fall down. What's going on?" He looked over Davey. "I thought you were—" *Hurt.* Mitch turned away, struggling with a temper he hadn't let go in years. A temper born of fear that shouldn't be his.

Davey wasn't his child. He had a mother. A mother who would soon leave and take Davey with her.

He felt a small hand grasp his. "I'm sorry, Mitch. Me and Mom were just tickling. I almost—" He pulled at Mitch's arm, trying to get him closer.

When Mitch bent closer, Davey whispered. "I almost told her about the porch. I didn't want to get you in trouble."

Mitch knelt before the boy, studying him closely. "Don't ever lie to your mother, Davey." He looked over the boy's head at her. "I'm the one who showed you. I don't care if she gets mad at me. But now that she's better, she's the one you have to listen to."

Her blue eyes softened in gratitude.

Mitch looked away. He didn't want her soft. He wanted her gone.

"Mitch—" Davey whispered earnestly. "Mom's gonna want me to take a bath."

A bath. Why hadn't he stopped to think about baths? Neither of them would be able to tolerate his daily dip into the icy mountain stream.

Davey looked disgusted.

"She's right, you know. You need one."

"Aw, Mitch—"

He stood up and looked at Perrie. "Sorry. I use the stream most days. But it's too—"

"Cold," she supplied, smiling fondly. "I know. I remember."

"I forget. You've lived here before."

Her lashes swept down, avoiding a topic difficult for both of them. "It's been a long time. Things change."

"Not around here."

Her eyes opened wide. "I'm glad to hear it. This place is special. Magic."

Then why didn't you come back when— Mitch quashed the question. The boy watched them, gaze avid. It was the first civil conversation they'd had.

He changed the subject. "I could rig you a shower outside, the way I do when I guide."

"Guide? You're an outfitter like Grandpa?"

He shrugged. "Sort of. I travel with the seasons. Should be in South Texas right now for dove and quail, but this would be the first winter Cy's place would be—"

Blue eyes went dark with grief. Tears glistened.

She wore her emotions on her sleeve. He could tell her it was the road to disaster.

Her voice was barely a whisper. "Where is he buried?"

He bit back the words of recrimination. "You know the grandfather spruce?"

Her gaze locked on his. "The one that looks out toward the sunrise?"

Mitch nodded. "I scattered his ashes there."

"I'm so glad. It was his favorite place."

If you knew that— Suddenly Mitch was back there, watching the man who'd cared when his own father had hated.... Watching Cy's eyes darken with pain and feeling so helpless...

Remembering the desperate three-hour trip he'd made into Cora to phone her. A call to grant the only wish that really meant anything to Cy. To see this woman...just once more.

Mitch glanced down at Davey. Cy would have loved him the most. But thanks to her neglect, Cy had never known Davey existed.

He looked back at the woman who'd refused to even come to the phone. He'd wanted to crawl through the phone lines to yank her out of her pampered, selfish existence. If Cy hadn't been so sick, Mitch would have gone to Boston and dragged her here himself.

Instead, he'd watched the man who'd brought him back from hell die alone. Unwanted by anyone but a man whom no one else wanted, either. Unmourned by his own blood.

He had to get out of here. Away from her.

The boy was leaning on his leg. He jerked his hand away from Davey's hair as if burned. For Davey's sake he had to clamp down on his contempt.

Voice carefully calm, he spoke to the child. "I'll be done in a few minutes. Can you wait for breakfast?"

Davey's blue eyes were clear and guileless. "Want me to help, Mitch? Mom, are you hungry?"

"I can fix your breakfast, sweetie."

"I said I'd fix it," Mitch snapped. "Get back into bed."

Then he turned on his heel and left, placing distance between him and the woman he did not understand.

Chapter Three

Perrie hadn't realized she'd fallen asleep again until the cabin door opened. Mitch stood there, clean shirt on—charcoal plaid this time—dark hair slicked back, gleaming like mink.

She saw his displeasure, quickly masked, that she was on the sofa instead of back in bed. But he didn't say anything, just turned and headed toward the kitchen.

He was so big. So powerful. So angry with her, yet he kept that anger carefully lashed under iron bands of control.

She could defuse that anger by explaining about Simon. But then she'd have to admit that she couldn't leave. Didn't know where to go.

He didn't want her here. He was a loner, down to the bone—of that she was sure. This place was his, even if by default. Cyrus Blackburn had loved this place and wouldn't have given it to him if he hadn't cared for Mitch. The Grandpa she knew would have ordered him off the place with a shotgun, let it rot from neglect before letting a stranger have it.

No, Mitch's grief was real. She had seen little emotion slip past his mask, but his grief and love for Grandpa were palpable.

And he'd helped them, never mind that he despised her. He'd been gentle with Davey, though it was obvious he had no experience with children.

But what would he say if he knew she was being hunted? Maybe he would help her, maybe not. She couldn't risk being thrown out until she was ready, until she had a plan.

Right now she couldn't clear her brain well enough to plan. All she could do was rest and get back her strength.

She would never go back. One escape, before Davey was conceived in violence, had taught her the price of Simon's displeasure. He was medieval in his thinking, cruel and unforgiving. On the cusp of a new century, she had lived as a chattel in a soft and pampered prison, forbidden contact with anyone from her old life. She would never forgive herself for her weakness.

He had left her alone after Davey's birth, lost interest in them both. Locked away in Simon's pretty prison while he played in the city, there had been no chances for escape until Simon himself had granted deliverance, divorcing her to marry someone else. But he had warned her to stay in Boston. She knew he had her watched and followed. As long as he had stayed away, she hadn't forced the issue. He seemed to have forgotten them.

Until the day that he showed up on her doorstep to claim the son he'd never loved, reminding her that Matheson power could wrest Davey away from her forever. She'd threatened him with going to the authorities with what she suspected about his money laundering, and Simon had only laughed, secure in his power. Then he turned the tables, telling her that if she breathed a word, he would take Davey somewhere that she would never find him.

Perrie had adopted her old subservient pose, groveling while rage ate a hole in her soul, knowing that he would do it, that she had to put his mind at ease. With the help of her only friend, Simon's wizened old gardener, Elias Conkwright, she laid the groundwork for leaving while making sure Davey was never alone with Simon until she could flee.

But one day Simon had picked Davey up from kindergarten unexpectedly. After two frantic days, Davey had returned—afraid.

It was a reminder of Simon's threat. Perrie knew then that she could not wait any longer. Time had run out, whether she had enough money or not. She wrote down everything she knew that could point toward Simon's white-collar crimes, and left the papers with Elias, who would deliver them not to the police, but to Boston's premier investigative reporter. She could only pray that someday justice would find Simon.

She had left the name of the town nearest her grandfather's cabin, asking Elias to contact her only in case of emergency—or if by some miracle, Simon was apprehended.

And she had fled to what she thought was safety.

Only to find a stranger in place of the man who would help.

Forcing away the whirling cloud of fear and despair, Perrie closed her eyes and sought the stillness that had helped her survive this far.

She would have to run again, it seemed.

But for now she would sleep.

"Mitch," Davey whispered, standing in the chair and stirring. "Want me to go wake Mom? It's almost ready."

Mitch took his gaze off the boy only long enough to check her, then shook his head. "We'll set it on the back. It'll keep warm for a while. Maybe she'll sleep longer."

Davey sighed, then wrinkled his face. "No one can sleep this much."

"Maybe not you, sport, but your mom's been very sick."

"When she gets better, can we take her fishing, too?"

"I can't imagine she'd like it."

"Oh, she would—she told me. Grandpa Cy used to take her fishing when she was my age."

He hated to disappoint the hopeful look in the boy's eyes. "Maybe. We'll have to see how long you're staying."

Davey's eyes widened. "We were gonna come live with Grandpa Cy, Mom told me." His brow wrinkled. "Maybe you don't want us to stay."

Too bright, the boy was. Of course he didn't want them to stay. He lived alone. Always had, except for visits to Cy. He moved from one guide job to the next, season to season. His home was his truck and the wide blue sky, the forests and rivers and streams.

But right now, eyes as blue as that sky were looking at him, vulnerable and lost. The boy needed some sense of security.

What the hell was she thinking, uprooting him like that? A child needed a safe place to grow up, to belong. Like he'd had, until—

"No use to worry about it now. Something will work out. Your oatmeal's ready." He scooped the boy into one arm and carried a bowl in the other, turning toward the table.

Perrie's soft, sleepy gaze studied him, and he felt like he'd been caught doing something illicit.

"Mom!" Davey crowed. "Look, I made oatmeal!" He glanced over at Mitch, sliding one arm around Mitch's neck. "Well, Mitch helped me, but mostly I made it."

"Enough for me?" Her voice held the huskiness of sleep, rasping its way along Mitch's nerves.

"Sure—" Davey squirmed to be let down. Mitch set him on his feet. "Look, you can have this bowl."

She rose, and Mitch could see that she wasn't yet steady on her feet. He started to go to her, but she cast him a forbidding glance, then straightened carefully, holding on to the arm of the sofa with one hand and using the other to free her braid of spun gold hair from her collar. With slow steps she rounded the sofa.

By the time she reached the table, what little color she had was gone. But her spine stayed ramrod straight and around her prickled a cloud of warning.

She wouldn't thank him to follow his instincts and carry her back to the bed. She wasn't his business, anyway—she'd only be here as long as it took to get her well enough to leave.

He'd turned down several jobs over this fall and winter. He'd disappointed some people; he was always in demand. But he'd felt the need to come—

Home.

No. Not home. He didn't need a home. Didn't want one. He'd merely come back to be sure Cy's cabin—his cabin—was all right for winter. He could leave tomorrow and get a job at the snap of his fingers. Maybe he should. Let her have the place if she wanted.

But the boy needed him right now. And so did

she—like it or not, wise or not. It wasn't in Jenny Gallagher's son to leave them stranded, not even a woman as heartless as this one.

Mitch finished dishing up Davey's oatmeal and his own. As he sat down, he couldn't help looking back through time to another table, another dark-haired man and blond woman and boy. All that was missing was the dark-haired older son who had once belonged at a table like this.

Who had once been part of a family.

Until he'd destroyed it.

Perrie woke at the sound of a thump on the kitchen floor, followed by a deep rumble and animated whispers. Her impulse to leap up from the bed and be sure Davey was all right was automatic, but she waited. Mitch was with him. No matter what he thought of her, she could not fault his care of her child.

Well, except maybe the lack of bathing. But Davey was no doubt in hog heaven.

The door opened a crack. A small blond head bobbed through the opening. When he saw that she was awake, he shoved through the door and bounced on the bed. "Mom—Mitch is making you a bath." His little face wrinkled in disgust. "He says I gotta take one after you're through."

"Good for him. You need one. I wonder if all little boys hate baths."

"They do," the deep voice confirmed.

Perrie glanced up at Mitch. "All of them?"

"My mom practically had to hog-tie my brother and me when we were kids." For a moment, he seemed younger, lighter of heart. The tawny eyes sparkled.

"You have a brother?" Davey asked. "Is he big like you?"

The sparkle vanished, replaced by a look of such deep sorrow that it hurt to watch.

Then the iron man recovered and resumed his careful mask. "I don't know." Mitch glanced at her, his expression neutral. "If you'd like to bathe, Cy had an old tub that should work."

He didn't know what his brother looked like? Perrie wanted to know more, but everything about him said *Back off*. The brief glimpse of a carefree boy was gone as if it had never existed. In its place was the forbidding stranger.

But forbidding or not, a bath sounded like heaven. Except that— "Where will you be?"

He snorted. "Davey and I will go outside."

Perrie fought a blush. No one but Simon had ever seen her naked. She wasn't sure she ever wanted to be seen by a man again. But this man...so overpowering...so male... He made her very conscious that she was female.

"I'm sorry. I sound ungracious. Thank you for going to so much trouble."

He shrugged. "Not that much."

She shook her head. "That's not how I remember it. Everything takes more work up here." Whatever the chasm between them, however much he wanted her gone, she owed him this much at least. More.

He had already turned to leave when she spoke up again. "Mitch—" He didn't turn back, but he stopped. "I want to thank you for everything you've done. Taking care of me—" She felt her face flame again as it dawned on her that he must have seen her naked. Someone had changed her sweat-soaked clothing and put her in the clothes that had been in her backpack. It couldn't have been Davey.

Resolutely she pressed on. "You've taken care of Davey, and I don't think—you don't have children, do you?"

He turned halfway, and she thought she saw fleeting amusement as he shook his head. "Not hardly."

"So much could have happened to him if I'd fallen ill and we'd been here alone—" Her throat tightened. Dire possibilities squeezed the breath out of her. Swallowing heavily, she shoved the terrifying prospects away, lifting her gaze to him once again. "I owe you more than I can ever repay."

She could swear that faint color stained his cheeks.

"Anyone would have done the same."

"No—no, they wouldn't have." This stranger had been kinder to her in these few days than her husband had been in their entire marriage.

Mitch watched her with careful eyes for a long moment. His voice turned gruff. "The water's going to get cold. Can you make it in there by your-self?''

Perrie wasn't sure, but she nodded anyway.

He glanced down at her son. ''Well, then, come on, Davey. Let's go outside.''

''Don't worry, Mom. Mitch will take care of us.'' Her son followed him out with not even a glance back at her, already chattering away happily. ''Can we watch for another eagle, Mitch?''

She'd never realized how hungry Davey was for a father.

Perrie watched them leave—the blond-haired owner of her heart and the dark giant who watched over them both.

He didn't want them here. At least, not her. Yet he took better care of both of them than the man who'd said sacred vows with her, who had fathered her son.

There had to be some way out of this coil. She would find it, somehow. For now her bath awaited.

Mitch stayed on the porch until he heard the wa-ter splash against the sides of the old washtub and he could be sure she'd made it all the way from the bedroom.

She couldn't drown—the tub wasn't that big. But she could have passed out along the way. She was far from recovered.

They wouldn't venture far, just in case. And he would try very hard not to think of ivory skin glis-tening with droplets of water. Of the slow track of moisture gliding down her slender spine toward gently rounded hips. Or of soap bubbles clinging to other silken curves.

Mitch tried to reconcile the soft, tender creature who loved her child so much with the woman who would refuse all contact with her only other living kin. Cy hadn't spoken of her much, but he'd told Mitch about Perrie's mother, about all the lovers. That Perrie had no idea who her father was.

She had reason to be wary of him, sure. He'd seen the fear in her eyes. He was a stranger and as far from her Boston life as anyone could be.

But she'd known Cy all her life, had spent big chunks of it here in this place. She had to know how much she meant to the old man, yet in his darkest hour she'd turned her back on him as though he meant nothing to her.

It had looked like real grief in her eyes when she spoke of Cy. She'd seemed genuinely shocked that he was dead. Either she was the finest actress he'd ever seen, or something was very wrong.

"Mitch?" Davey ran back to him, breathless. "Come see! I found a squirrel."

"If you're this noisy, he'll be long gone." But Mitch rose to follow the child, enjoying his excitement. The fresh eyes Davey cast on the world never ceased to amaze him. He was too fearless by half, but no more so than Mitch himself had been as a child. Yet, within the fearless boy was an old man, a child aged before his time.

Perrie was hiding something. Maybe this boy

knew what it was, but Mitch wouldn't stoop to that.
Instead of daydreaming about glistening wet curves,
Mitch should start asking the owner of those curves
some hard questions.

Perrie jerked awake from the nightmare, heart
beating a fandango. She rubbed a slow circle on her
chest and breathed deeply, staring into the darkness,
listening. When she heard Davey's even breathing
from the cot nearby, she relaxed a little, but she
knew sleep would be elusive.

She wasn't sure where Mitch was now; caught
up in the bedtime ritual with Davey, she'd lost track
of where she'd heard him last. It didn't matter. She
couldn't stay in the darkness one second longer.

She tightened the belt of her robe and slipped
through the door into the main room, headed for
the firelight's glow.

A few steps into the room, she stopped dead in
her tracks. Stretched out on the floor in front of the
dying fire, Mitch lay sound asleep.

Perrie approached with slow, careful steps. She'd
never seen him like this, hard features softened in
slumber.

He looked younger, less careworn. The fierce eagle eyes closed, his frame still conveyed power and
strength, but the man before her seemed almost vulnerable.

She'd never met anyone so alone. Her grandfather had spent much of his life in these mountains
by himself, his solitude punctuated by stints as a

hunting and fishing guide. Grandpa had been alone, but never lonely. Solitude was very much a part of who he was, intertwined almost at a cellular level with his sense of humor, his love of the wilderness, his blue eyes.

Something about Mitch was different. It was almost as if solitude were not a choice but a defense.

He didn't know what his brother looked like. What was his story? Where was his family? Had he known gentleness in his life or only sorrow?

Sorrow. That was it. Beneath the power, beneath the fierce determination, the harsh strength, Perrie sensed a deep well of sorrow in this man. Why? What had happened? What had he suffered that made him so fiercely protective of his shell, so rigidly controlled?

But Davey breached those high walls. Something in the boy touched the man and mined the goodness his manner hid.

He wasn't accustomed to children and his methods might not be found in any parenting book, but he had been good to a child thrust upon him by circumstance. Had taken care of a child not his own, had not punished the child for the mother's believed sins.

He did not want her here, could not wait for her to leave. But he had still granted her more kindness in a few days than she had had from Simon in years.

Perrie's mind whirled, trying to sort out the best path. This cabin had been her lodestone, her guiding star for so long that she'd never considered what to do next, where she might go.

Perhaps if she were another woman, more suited to passion, it might be possible for her to seduce him. He already cared for Davey; if he found passion with her, would he want them to stay?

But she wasn't that woman, and she had sold herself once. Never again. Never mind that she hadn't known she was selling her soul until it was too late—she would never erase the loathing she felt for a girl so confused and weak-minded that she had not seen Simon for who he was. Blinded by the fairy tale she wanted her life to become, the little secretary wooed by the heir apparent had been caught up in a whirlwind of illusion.

She knew now that her allure for Simon had been that she was so malleable. So stupid and needy and eager to become the woman he wanted. She would never erase the shame of being that girl who never saw the trap coming until it was too late. Who kept believing it was her fault and things might change if only she could do everything right.

That girl was dead. The woman who replaced her had been forged in the fires of hate.

She would die before she let Simon take her child. He might have the deck stacked with his family's connections and wealth, but somehow she would elude him. Somehow she would win.

You can't prove anything, Perrie. And who would believe you over me? Don't even try—not unless you want to lose the boy forever. With effort, she shoved Simon's words away. She had to think, not panic.

She had little money left and her strength was not yet returned. For a time longer, she had to tiptoe through the days and pray that Mitch would not make them leave. She did not know enough about him to tell him her story yet.

Perrie rubbed her arms against the chill. Tending the dying fire would wake him.

She spotted an old quilt folded on top of a chest. Tiptoeing quietly, she retrieved it and moved to Mitch's side.

Holding her breath, she covered the sleeping man.

I promise I won't involve you any more than I must, to save my son.

He shifted slightly. Before he could awaken and ask her questions she could not afford to answer, Perrie rose. Making her way back into the waiting darkness, she prayed she would find her own answer soon.

Chapter Four

In that half-world between sleep and waking, Mitch wondered what was different. Unlike his usual snap to attention, something held him in a softer, sweeter place—a place he had not been in all the years past since that one fateful rainy night.

For just one moment, he could almost hear laughter, almost feel the warm glow of belonging. His eyelids heavy, he cast his thoughts toward the elusive tendrils of the place that had once been home. He rolled over to his side and pulled the quilt—

Quilt. Mitch awoke and frowned. He was lying in front of the dying fire in Cy's cabin. With a quilt spread over him.

For one traitorous second, Mitch remembered being tucked into bed as a child, remembered the sense of safety and order, of being wrapped in the arms of love. He squeezed his eyes shut tightly, hoping to sleep again and recapture just one more fleeting moment.

But sleep had fled, and with it illusion. He hadn't been a child for many years. And he had lost all right to love through his own failings. He had killed the woman who had loved him from birth, and he had been banished—and even that wasn't payment enough. What he had done to destroy his family could not be put right.

So he lived alone.

And he would live alone again, once they were gone, the boy who reminded him so much of Boone…and the fragile woman who had covered him with a quilt.

They could not leave soon enough. He was ready, more than ready, to knit silence around him once more. He had talked more in the last two days than in the last two years. He could not need, could not let himself want more than he had. The peace he had reached had required years to build and in a matter of days, the boy and his mother had breached his walls. Where quiet stillness had reigned, now too much lay tumbled like a fallen house of blocks.

Mitch shoved to his feet, throwing the quilt aside with a muttered curse. He strode to the window and scowled, seeing that it was still full darkness outside.

Pacing the floor like a caged beast, he wanted nothing more than to walk away, to seek the stillness of the forest, to lose himself in the call of a bird, the rustle beneath the branches. To think of nothing more than the tracks on the ground before him, to become not a man but simply a thread in the fabric of nature. Nature had no expectations to betray. Mother Earth simply was. You learned her many faces and you stayed alert to stay alive. In the keen pitch of attention she required, the world of people, of pain and loss, could not compete. Could not torment.

But even as he craved that immersion, Davey's little face rose before him, blue eyes alight with the magic of seeing the forest through new and innocent eyes. For one sweet second, Mitch imagined that the boy was his, imagined guiding the child to manhood. Swiftly, like an assassin, longing pierced, needle sharp.

Mitch abruptly turned from the window and faced the door of the room where they slept, the golden-haired, faithless mother and her child. No matter what he wanted, no matter how much he longed to walk away, he would not. She was too weak yet, the boy too small, this place too remote and wild.

As soon as she was stronger, he would know why Perrie was here and when she would leave. When he could be alone again.

But for now he would watch over them both.

From a distance.

Mitch picked up the quilt and folded it, trying to shake off the image of delicate hands touching him while he slept.

"Mom, what about the new story?"

Perrie lay back against the sofa cushions, wondering about Mitch. He'd been gone most of the day, and now they'd finished supper and he hadn't appeared yet.

"Mom? Did you hear me?"

She pulled her gaze from the doorway and took Davey's chin in her hand. "I'm barely started on it."

"That's okay. Sometimes you take a long time."

He was right about that. Sometimes the stories took weeks, even longer. She'd had little time or energy since before they left to begin a new one. Truth be told, she wasn't ready now. But Davey had accepted so much change in his life; this she would not deny him.

She'd always spun stories for herself as a child, then for Davey. It was a pleasure they shared, a gift she could give him. Even through the years after she'd discovered the nightmare of marriage to Simon, she'd been able to hold on to the refuge of her stories. She'd known it would be the final defeat if she let Simon kill that part of her, so she'd held on for dear life. The stories and Davey had been the only color in the prison she'd entered the day she married the man she'd thought was her prince.

"This one might take a while," she said. "Ermengilda's a complicated girl."

Davey giggled. "What a dumb name!"

Perrie lifted her chin playfully. "She can't help the name she was given. She's a princess, even if she looks like a trout."

"A trout? Like the one I caught?"

"This is a very special fish, much too clever to be caught."

"Mitch could do it. I know he could."

Perrie frowned slightly. Davey shouldn't get attached.

Davey laughed, blue eyes shining. "A girl fish named Ermen—"

"Ermengilda."

"I can call her Ermie."

"Oh no, you can't, young man. She's a princess, and a princess would never have a nickname like Ermie."

"I'm glad I'm not a princess. Davey's a better name, anyway."

She grabbed him around the waist with one hand, tickling his ribs with the other. "Not for a princess."

His knees buckled under him. But gamely he reached for her ribs.

She was ticklish, too.

For as long as she could summon the strength, they played, each seeking to avoid the other's fingers but grasping for tender places. Much too quickly, Perrie had to cry uncle.

"Okay, okay, you win." Falling back against the pillows, she felt her head spin.

Davey rose above her, towheaded hair sticking out all over the place, sweaty curls around his scalp. Leaping to his feet, he danced around, arms lifted in victory. "Yeah, I win! I'm the champion!"

"Watch it, buster. Losers don't like telling stories to winners who gloat."

He turned a much-too-wise smile on her. "You like telling me stories."

Reaching up to pull him close, she cradled him against her body, already conscious of how much he was growing…how soon he'd be too big to want this. "You know me too well."

Outside the cabin, Mitch stood in the shadows, watching the two golden heads together through the window. He had heard their laughter from across the clearing, and it had called him like a siren. He would listen to this story and see what he might learn about this woman who had so many different faces.

Perrie snuggled Davey's bony shoulders closer, smoothing his tousled blond hair. Their tussle had released that boy scent—a little sweet, a little sharp, a little of sweaty socks—the smell that seemed to be Davey's alone.

She began the story.

"Ermengilda Trout was sure she was a princess. Of course, there were no mirrors in the river so she couldn't be certain that her hair was long and flowing or her eyes looked like sparkling jewels. Henry Sunfish told her she was just an ugly old girl, but her mother smiled and said her scales shone beautifully in the sun.

"Bernie the Catfish, never very talkative, simply said, 'Nothin' wrong with dreamin', child.'

"Ermengilda knew they were all wrong. She *was* a princess, and someday she would show them. Her prince would come and rescue her. He'd see past her scales and tail and bugging eyes, see inside her to the heart that beat strong and brave and true.

"One day, she and Henry were playing. She looked up through water bright with sunlight. Up past teasing dragonflies. Up and straight into the face of what must surely be the Prince of the Pretty People.

"'Pretty?' Henry snorted. 'He has no tail, you dumb old girl. He's got stupid stringy black things sprouting from his head. His scales have no color. And his eyes—' here Henry shuddered 'They're— eck—blue.'"

"Hey," Davey complained, sitting up slightly. "My eyes are blue."

"Shh," Perrie urged. "Listen to what she says."

"Okay." He subsided, snuggling back down, his eyes growing heavy once more.

"Like mine, thought Ermengilda. Like my princess eyes. Maybe he's the one. The one who'll see me as I am.

"But to Henry she merely replied, 'That black stuff is called hair, silly. He has black hair.'

"'What use is that?' Henry protested. 'It will only—eeek!' He screamed and darted away from the giant arm that had plunged into the water.

"'Swim, Ermengilda—swim for your life!'

"But she couldn't," Perrie said. "Because fingers were already tickling her tummy and she was laughing too hard to move."

"Fish can't laugh," Davey interrupted. "Can they?"

"Are you so sure?"

"Uh-uh," he replied sleepily.

"Well, Ermengilda's no ordinary fish, you see."

"So what happens next?"

"I don't know. I was thinking about adding kissing and stuff."

"Eck," replied Davey. "Gross."

"I don't guess there has to be kissing, but usually when princes save princesses there's at least a little kissing going on."

"Could there be a sword fight first?"

Perrie smiled. "Who's the prince going to fight?"

"The bad guy." He opened his eyes again. "There's got to be a bad guy, right, Mom?"

"Maybe."

"Sure there does, so the prince can rescue the princess." His eyes were closing, his voice growing soft. "I would rescue you, Mom, 'cause you're like a princess."

She stroked the hair of the child who held her heart in his small hands, and tried not to cry. In a voice less steady than she would like, she whispered to her now-sleeping child.

"I know you would, sweetheart."

Then she kissed his forehead and tucked the quilt around him on the sofa. She made a feeble attempt to lift him, but he was getting too heavy for her to carry even when she was well. When Mitch came back, she'd ask him to help her. She sank down before the fire and stared into the flames.

She'd wished for her own prince for many years, but she'd made a mistake when she thought she'd found him. Being a romantic was dangerous, Perrie had learned.

Life wasn't a fairy tale, she knew that. She would raise Davey to be smart and strong and wiser than she had been.

But with all her heart she wanted a part of Davey never to have to give up his innocence. She had to find a way to protect both him and his dreams from a father who would destroy both.

She could only hope she would be enough.

Mitch turned away from the window and stared into the darkness, locked into place by memory. Another mother's voice echoed in his head, and for a moment he could almost feel the warmth where he was tucked into her side. Could remember delicate fingers stroking his hair as she read him a story and he fought the claim of sleep, never dream-

ing a day would come when he would not be protected by that golden web of love.

Perrie shouldn't be filling Davey's head with all
those romantic notions. It would only make it
harder for him when the world outside destroyed
them.

He turned back to see her tenderly tuck the quilt
around the boy, then try to lift him. His muscles
tensed to go inside to help her, but when she pulled
her arms away and settled in front of the fire, he
turned his attention to the dark night, the stars
winking past the treetops.

He would take care of carrying Davey, but not
yet. Not while she was so close, in a cabin that was
shrinking by the day.

When he turned back, she had curled up on her
side in front of the fire, her breathing slow and
deep.

Oh, hell. Now he'd have to carry her, too. The
only thing he wanted less than to be near her was
to have to touch her.

Shaking his head, Mitch sighed and straightened.
He entered the cabin and stood there for a minute,
watching them sleep like two innocents. Then
Davey snored softly, and Mitch smiled, crossing the
floor to pick him up.

When he did, Davey frowned slightly, then snuggled closer, his head pressed into Mitch's chest.
Something inside Mitch did a slow revolution, and
he knew that though he couldn't wait for them to
leave, he would miss this child.

But that couldn't be helped. And the sooner they left, the sooner he could get on with his life. With long strides, he carried Davey to his cot and tucked the quilt around him. For one moment, his hand hovered over the tousled golden hair, close enough to touch. But he didn't.

"Sleep well," Mitch whispered. Then he turned away and tried to decide which would be worse, to have to touch Perrie to carry her, or to have to talk to her if she were awake and could take herself to bed.

There, before the fire, he stood over her and studied the woman who was a mystery to him. Her ever-present braid lay limply behind her on the rug, and he wondered how it would look, loosened so that the curls making constant bids for escape were freed. For just a moment, he tried to imagine her, golden waves cascading over her shoulders and down her back, blue eyes alight with laughter and looking at him like—

Mitch cursed beneath his breath, and Perrie stirred, a tiny frown appearing between delicate brows. The purple shadows smudging her eyes had receded, but exhaustion still lined her face.

Wondering was foolish. Even if she woke up and gave him a perfectly good reason why she'd been so callous to Cy, it wouldn't matter. He wanted no one in his life. Needed no one. That was how it had been for sixteen years, and how it would continue. Some people were simply meant to be alone.

Before she could awaken, Mitch knelt on the

floor and scooped her into his arms, simply a burden to carry like a stack of firewood or a load of supplies. He rose to his feet.

She stirred softly and nestled closer, turning that china doll face into his chest, the golden braid falling from her shoulder. Her hand grasped the front of his shirt for an endless second, and she whimpered faintly. Mitch's own hands tightened around her, all too aware of her bottom against one arm, her slender back against the other beneath the thin layers of cloth. He froze, barely breathing, willing her to continue sleeping.

But something of his tension must have communicated itself to her. Slowly, dark lashes swept upward, blinking once...twice. Eyes as blue as a mountain lake looked at him with unprotected softness for a span of time that was only a second or two but could have been years. Her hand tightened again against his shirt, and he felt her touch like a brand on his body. Desire rose, swift and shocking, and it was all Mitch could do not to drop her like a hot potato.

For endless seconds, he felt the blue eyes look into his as though she could see down to the bottom of his shriveled soul. And no matter what he knew or what he believed, he could not look away, nor could he speak.

Then her lashes flickered and her eyes closed.

And like a prisoner who has seen a glimpse of sunlight from the dungeon, Mitch felt forgotten yearning shudder through him. Averting his mind's eye from the sight, he took her to her bed and escaped the room with all haste.

Behind the closed door of his own bedroom, Mitch drew in his first deep breath of the night.

Perrie awoke, blinking against the strong bars of sunlight, butter-yellow and making the log walls glow golden. She stretched, then glanced over to see Davey's cot empty. Listening for sounds to indicate that he and Mitch were inside, she heard nothing.

Mornings were already cold. Sweeping the quilt aside, she glanced down at the thick socks on her feet. By all rights, they should be able to stand by themselves, she'd had them on so long. She needed to get to the car to get more clothes but as she stood up, she quickly realized that she was far from ready to walk the two miles.

Making her way across the room, Perrie paused by the tall pine chest that flanked the doorway, running her hands across the surface of it, still covered with that same strip of once-bright Mexican cloth. Her mind's eye returned to the past when she couldn't see to the top of the chest, could only see the edges of the cloth's fringe. Grandpa Cy had finally asked her one day what she was staring at so intently.

He'd laughed when she'd told him that she wondered what was up there. Picking her up, he let her look where she had imagined treasures. Instead, she'd found little. Change from his pocket. A photo of her mother as a girl. Perrie's own school picture, her front tooth missing. And a dark, grainy photo of Cy and his beloved Madeline, the grandmother she'd never known.

They hadn't seemed treasures to her then, but now she wished with all her heart to see them just once more.

Maybe Mitch— She shook her head. Would he have kept them? Likely not.

Perrie swept her fingers over the carved square wooden pulls of the top drawer, wondering if the chest contained her grandfather's things, or Mitch's. Had he given up this room to them or made the second bedroom his own? Her fingers hovered over the pull.

No. It wasn't right. She was a guest here, nothing more. Maybe she'd come here expecting to be family, but that was not the reality she'd found. Sliding her fingers across the rough wood, she turned away and headed for the living room.

Sunlight flooded through the small window over the sink in the kitchen area to her left. Straight ahead, the window beside the front door was shadowed by the porch, but more sunlight brightened the living area from the window off to her right. In the fireplace, flames crackled.

On the old oak kitchen table, the torn edge of a brown paper sack stood against the salt shaker. "Davey's with me" it read in a bold, masculine scrawl.

No signature, but none was needed. The handwriting was like the man, strong and to the point. Not one superfluous word. She smiled. Mitch guarded words as though he couldn't replace the ones he used.

At least he'd thought to prevent her worry. *Mitch will take care of us, Mom.* Her smile vanished. Davey had opened his heart to Mitch, but she couldn't. He was too full of contradictions, too much a mystery.

Just for a moment, an image darted across her mind. Strong arms beneath her, hard chest against her cheek. The smell of a man's sweat and wood smoke and piney forest. Eyes burning amber locked on hers.

A wish to know their pain, the source of the dark shadows. To burrow closer and lose herself in their depths.

Shivering at the memory, Perrie moved near the fireplace to snag the quilt she'd used to cover Mitch, wrapping it around her. With brisk steps, she headed for the woodstove and poured herself a cup of the coffee he had left warming on the back.

Stay busy, Perrie. Make yourself useful. And stay out of his way.

In the corner, she saw a barrel Mitch used to store water. She checked the reservoir on the right side of the woodstove, finding it already full of still-warm water. She would wash herself with it, then heat more.

Then she'd wash their clothes and scrub away foolish thoughts in the process.

* * *

"How come you don't have a TV, Mitch?" Davey asked from his perch on Mitch's back.

The boy had lasted longer than Mitch had expected, hiking a good mile and a half without complaint. Probably closer to three miles, if you counted all the times he'd darted off to the side to find some new treasure. And he'd asked at least a million questions. Maybe two.

"Don't need one."

Davey fell silent, but it was that kind of silence that was almost loud with all the brain clicking Mitch could see going on.

Sure enough, it didn't take long. "So you don't miss seeing Power Rangers?"

Mitch turned his head to the side. "What's that?"

Davey's fingers tightened on his shoulders. "Oh, wow, you should see them. They're regular kids but they've got these special powers and they wear these cool suits with helmets. My favorite one is the Blue Ranger."

"Hmmmph." Cartoons, he guessed. "You heard of Jim Bridger? This wilderness is named after him. He discovered the Great Salt Lake and was one of the first white men to see Yellowstone. Traveled this part of the country when it was still wild, when it belonged to the animals and the Indians."

"Real Indians?"

"Yep. Crow and Shoshone, mostly."

"Did Grandpa Cy know him?"

Mitch smiled. "No, Cy wasn't even born then.

This was way back over a hundred and fifty years ago, back when there were no roads or cabins. A long, long time before TVs or cars.''

Mitch was quiet for a moment. ''But Cy was a lot like him. He loved these mountains. He built that cabin with his own hands. Built the furniture inside it, too.''

''Didn't he get lonesome?''

Mitch's mood darkened. *Not until the end. Not until your mother wouldn't come.* ''He liked his own company fine. And he had all the animals, had plenty of Mother Nature to keep him entertained.''

''Did Jim Bridger kill animals?'' Davey's voice turned slightly sharp. ''I don't think that's nice.''

''This is hard country, son. A man had to kill to eat.''

''They could go to the grocery store. They didn't have to hurt the animals.''

Mitch pulled Davey from his back and set him on the ground at his feet. Then he knelt and met the boy's eyes squarely. ''They didn't have grocery stores. Wyoming was wild then. A man had to find his own food.''

''I don't want anybody hurting animals.''

''It's part of nature, but you don't do it to hurt them. You only take what you need to survive, and you thank the animal for its sacrifice. Some Indians believed that you took the animal's spirit inside you and it became a part of you. We're not separate from the animals, Davey. We're all part of the same earth.''

Davey's eyes studied him, troubled. His voice went very low. "Have you killed animals, Mitch?" His look made it clear that the truth would be the wrong answer.

But it was the truth. A man faced it and dealt with the consequences. "Yes, I have."

The boy frowned, looking mutinous. "That's a bad thing to do."

"Was it bad for you to catch that fish?"

"I—I didn't like that sharp hook. I bet it hurt."

"The world's not a fairy tale, Davey. It's a cycle of death and rebirth. Trees die and fall to the ground, then insects eat them and they crumble and fertilize the soil for new trees to feed on and grow. Bigger animals eat smaller animals. Nature is a balance, and we're part of that balance. Cars and airplanes and TVs may seem natural to you, but they don't belong in the true balance of nature. Man is taking over the natural places that the animals need to survive, just so he can have his pretty toys.

"Most of those who lived here long ago only hunted for what they needed to survive. That's why this wilderness is here now, to help the animals who can't compete with the world of cars and TVs. But even here, coyotes eat the old and weak elk who fall behind the herd. Birds eat insects. Fish eat insects, too. Birds eat fish."

"I don't want to kill animals." Davey looked troubled.

"Maybe you'll never need to. I wouldn't want you to do it if it wasn't your wish. But if you ever do want to hunt, I hope you'll do it right. Some hunting is necessary to keep overpopulation down, but don't do it to excess. Use equipment that tests your skill and gives the animal a fair chance. Use the parts of the animal as fully as you can, not just for some trophy on your wall.'' Mitch thought about the clients he'd culled because they didn't understand, were trigger-happy or just wanted something to show off.

"And always thank the animal for its sacrifice and dedicate yourself to keeping its spirit alive. Make its bravery part of you. Let its life force live on.''

"I wish I had thanked my fish,'' Davey whispered.

Mitch's heart squeezed. He resisted the urge to pull the child close. He held back the smile that threatened. "You still can.''

Blue eyes went wide. "He could still hear me?''

Did he know that for sure? "I think so. Somewhere, a part of all creatures lives on.''

"Even Grandpa Cy?''

Sorrow struck Mitch like a blow he hadn't seen coming. Cy would have loved this child so much. Damn Perrie for keeping the boy away until it was too late.

But blue eyes were watching, waiting for an answer.

"Yes.'' Mitch had no doubt of this. The old man's spirit hovered in every inch of these woods.

"I think Grandpa Cy can hear you if you want to talk."

"I'm gonna go tell Mom. She's really sad that he's gone." Davey looked ready to run back to the cabin. "Can we go back now and tell her?"

No, he wanted to say. *You go on. I don't want to be anywhere near her.*

But he didn't say it. Rising, he turned to lead the way back, noticing the clouds moving in, heavy and darker than the ones that brought the sporadic afternoon showers, a deeper gunmetal-gray. Mitch resisted the urge to groan.

It could snow any day of the year here, even in the middle of summer. Early October wasn't too soon at all, but the last thing he wanted was a new reason for them to stay or for him to need to stay with them.

Sometimes Mother Nature was a coldhearted witch.

"Come on, son. We've got a storm rolling in." Mitch pulled Davey up on his back and took off with quick steps.

Chapter Five

Perrie fastened the sheet more tightly around her waist, securing it with one of the clothespins she'd been using, wishing she had longer legs and it weren't trailing the floor behind her. Thank goodness for the clothespins—and that Mitch had left them right where Grandpa had kept them. She wished she could take off the T-shirt she wore and wash it, too, but she had nothing else to put on. Maybe Mitch would loan her something, but she wasn't about to look through his belongings.

She had felt enough like an intruder, going into his room to gather up the neat stack of dirty clothes he'd placed on a stool in the corner. She'd hesitated at the doorway, uneasy about entering the room that resembled a monk's cell more than anything. But in the end, she couldn't be rude enough to wash their clothes and not his.

One more garment to wring out by hand and hang on the line outside that Grandpa had strung years ago. Then she could sit down. Before she fell down.

Drawing in a deep breath, she twisted and squeezed again, thankful it wasn't Mitch's jeans this time. Those had taken every ounce of her too-watery muscles. The man had some very long legs.

The cabin door opened suddenly. "What the devil are you doing?" Mitch's voice boomed out.

Perrie didn't turn, just kept twisting and squeezing. "I should think it would be obvious."

Then he was at her side, removing the shirt from her hands. His strong fingers finished the job with quick, efficient motions. "Go sit down," he grated.

"What are you doing, Mom?"

Perrie turned toward her son's voice. "Washing our clothes."

"Take your mom over to the couch, Davey. She needs to sit down."

Perrie bristled at being ordered around like a child. She glanced up at the man whose shoulder she barely reached, seeing eyes gone stormy. "I'm not a child. I don't need a keeper."

"Could have fooled me. Now go sit down or I'll carry you there myself."

For a split second, she remembered being carried last night. Remembered leaning into that broad chest. She hadn't dreamed that, nor the need she'd felt to know what turned those eyes so dark with sorrow.

And for another brief flicker, she saw that he remembered it, too. A muscle flexed in his strong jaw. His nostrils flared. Stormy eyes glowed hot—

Perrie stepped back, reaching for Davey's shoulder. Turning too quickly, she stumbled over the trailing edges of the sheet, the awkward movement jerking the fabric down and popping the clothespin off. Grasping at the sheet with one hand, she reached for the edge of the sink with the other.

Strong hands pulled her upright, up against a hard, powerful frame.

With a gasp, Perrie felt the pressure of breast to ribs, hip to belly. She lifted her gaze in shock to see the same awareness in him.

She drew herself back with exquisite care, pulling the sheet tightly between her breasts, still feeling spark-shot and shaky.

Perrie forced herself to straighten. "Our clothes were dirty. They needed washing."

"Me and Mitch could go to the car and get our other clothes, couldn't we, Mitch?"

Mitch tore his gaze away from Perrie, glancing down at her son. "There's a storm coming. You stay here and help your mom." For all the fury in his eyes when he looked at her, his tone was gentle with Davey.

"Okay." Davey sighed. "Come on, Mom. You

need to sit down like Mitch said.'' He reached for her hand.

She'd had enough of this hero worship. ''Mitch doesn't know what either one of us needs.''

The hurt look on Davey's face made her feel churlish, but she was tired of Mitch's high-handed manner. She'd had enough of men telling her how to live her life. ''Excuse me, please. I'll be in the other room.'' Turning to go, she tripped again on the sheet and muttered furiously under her breath as she pulled it up from beneath her feet.

Amusement threaded through Mitch's voice. ''You want to borrow something else to put on?''

She didn't want to see a smug look on his face. ''I'll be fine.''

''I've got to bring in those clothes from outside and dry them in front of the fire. It could be a while.''

Her bare feet were already cold. Her legs had chill bumps from the draft where the sheet parted. But she still didn't want to ask any more favors.

Until she looked down and saw that the increasing chill had puckered her nipples. Inhaling sharply, she pulled the sheet up over her breasts. She couldn't stay huddled inside it all day.

With a proud toss of her head, she turned to face him, scrupulously polite. ''I suppose that makes sense.'' Even to her own ears, she sounded ungracious.

One dark eyebrow cocked.

"I apologize. I just—" *Can't lean on anyone else. Not any longer.*

He didn't comment, just waited for her to finish. Her discomfort increased.

Perrie shook her head, then rubbed her temple. "I'm not a very good patient. I'm used to being the caretaker, not the one who needs care."

His eyes held what might be sympathy. "Don't much like relying on others myself." He dropped the wet shirt onto the counter and moved past her. "I'll get you something."

Davey walked over and took her hand. This time she didn't balk. "Mitch is okay, Mom. He's not like my dad."

From the mouths of babes... She knelt before him, gripping his hand tightly and speaking softly. "Don't get too attached, Davey. Mitch lives alone and he likes it that way."

Davey's chin jutted. "He likes me, Mom. I know he does. Don't you like him?"

"It's not that, honey. It's just that—" *I'm running for my life. Your life.* But she couldn't explain that to him. How would he feel if he knew the true evil of which his father was capable? Just the tiny glimpse he'd had of Simon's cruelty had scared him badly. Something inside Perrie balked at having to tell her beloved son that the man whose blood he shared was evil. Instead, she'd simply told him they would be staying with Grandpa Cy for a while, that though it was very different from the city, it was a good, safe place.

She was spared a response when Mitch returned. She kissed Davey and whispered, "We'll be okay." Grasping the sheet firmly, she rose.

"It's nothing fancy. I figured sweats would be the easiest thing to adjust to how much smaller you are."

"They'll be fine. I'm very grateful. If you'll give me a minute, I'll help you with the clothes on the line."

"Your hair is still wet. Stay inside. Then you can give me your car keys and I'll go get whatever you need."

"Mitch, I can—"

He glanced back over his shoulder, frowning. "If it were Davey, you'd be telling him to go back to bed." His gaze dared her to argue.

Suddenly she felt the strength drain right out of her. She sighed. "You're right. I just—"

His voice was oddly gentle. "Don't like being a patient. I heard. But you have to rest to get well."

What he didn't say was even clearer to both of them. She needed to get well enough to leave.

But she had to hold to one point. "I am not getting back in that bed."

"Suit yourself." He shrugged and reached for his jacket. When he opened the door, she could feel how much the temperature had dropped. He left without a backward glance.

Davey looked ready to leap to Mitch's defense.

"Not a word, young man." She pointed a finger at him. "I'll be right back."

* * *

First Mitch moved more wood to the porch of the cabin. Good thing he'd been splitting extra. Looked like they would need it.

As he wheeled another load from the woodpile, his thoughts drifted to how he'd found her. She looked like a little girl playing dress-up, the sheet wrapped several times around her small frame, bare toes peeking from beneath it, her face with barely more color than the white cotton. He'd felt a strong urge to gather her up against him, to wrap his hands around those small feet and warm them.

But she was anything but a girl, small stature or not. She might be thin from the effects of her illness right now, but she still had a woman's curve to her hips. And the nipples that puckered so prettily crowned breasts that would nicely fill even his big hands. She was small, but she was all woman.

And the last thing he needed was to be stuck in a cabin with her while this storm blew through.

He cast a glance at the sky, then at the wood. Enough for now—he had winter gear and might need an excuse to get outside all too soon, anyway.

With quick steps, he walked to the line where she'd hung the clothes she'd so painstakingly washed. When he pulled his jeans off the line, he shook his head. They were still soaking wet, but how had those small hands ever wrung them out in the first place?

Then he reached her panties and bras, and his hand stilled. Though he'd taken them off her when he was trying to bring down her fever, he hadn't really paid attention. Now he touched the lace, the tiny triangles of silky fabric. Heat flared through him, racing down nerve paths too long dormant.

With a ripe curse, Mitch snatched them from the line and added them to his bundle, focusing only on clothespins the rest of the way.

He stalked toward the cabin, pushing the door open.

Perrie's head jerked up from where she'd set a chair before the fire. When she met his gaze, color rushed into her face.

"Mitch! Look at Mom." Davey giggled. "Your clothes are too big."

That was an understatement. She'd had to roll the legs up so many times that they formed an inner tube around her ankles. The bulky rolls at her wrists were the same. With her hair still wet, she looked like a half-drowned waif.

A beautiful, self-conscious waif.

Treat her like she's Davey. Like she's a child who needs tending for a while.

Not like a woman. Anything but a woman.

"Here—" He dropped the pile of wet clothing on the kitchen table. "I'll get a rope to string across the room." He left the cabin.

Fast.

Perrie watched him go, then turned toward the fire to dry her hair. In minutes, he was back with a length of rope, nails and a hammer. His face closed in like shutters had been latched, he quickly and efficiently strung a clothesline from one wall of the living area, crossing in front of the fire and extending to the kitchen wall.

She turned toward the pile of clothing.

He moved up beside her. ''Go sit down.''

She bristled. ''I can do this.''

He muttered darkly and pulled the top garment, a pair of his jeans, off the pile.

He was too close. Perrie wanted to back away.

Then she grabbed a shirt next. Beneath it lay a pair of her panties.

She grabbed for them at the same time he reached into the pile. Their hands brushed. It felt like someone had touched her with a live wire.

She gasped faintly and jerked back, her gaze jumping to his.

Dark eyes turned darker, meeting hers for a second that felt incandescent. A muscle leapt in his jaw.

''Here,'' he almost growled, holding out the pink scrap to her.

The sight of her panties in his hands did something to her insides. Shot down her veins as hot as the blaze she felt in her cheeks. Perrie grabbed for the pink lace and stuffed it under the shirt she was holding.

''If you think you can hang these up, I'll head for your car.'' He bit off every word as though it cost him to utter each one.

She didn't look at him. "You don't have to do that."

"You sure as hell can't. Give me the keys."

"You don't know where I parked."

"I'm a tracker. I'll find it."

"I don't—"

"Hiding something?"

Oh, no. They couldn't have this discussion.

"No," she said quickly. "I just—it's a lot of trouble for you, that's all."

"This storm could last one day or several. You want to be washing those out every day?"

She didn't have to look to know what "those" were. Her fingers tightened around the wet bundle in her arms.

No, she didn't want to have to do that. It wasn't a problem to hang them out in front of Davey. He had long dismissed them as just underwear, no different from his Winnie the Pooh briefs. But now with Mitch around, leaving them out would be like waving a red flag in front of a bull.

And it wasn't like she had anything in the car but clothes and toys, anyway. Just that there was so much, more than most people would take on a simple visit.

She didn't have to tell him anything. He didn't like talking, anyway. And soon they'd be gone.

That thought made her stomach clench. She still didn't know where they'd go. But it looked like she had a few days' reprieve, thanks to Mother Nature.

"I'll get my car keys." She turned to leave.

"You've got a wet spot on the front of the sweat-shirt." His voice sounded faintly amused. "You can leave the pile here. I've already seen what there is to see."

He could mean not only her underwear but also her body. Her face still uncomfortably warm, she dropped the clothes back on the pile and headed toward her pack.

Perrie thrust the keys in his hands, then busied herself hanging up laundry while he disappeared into his room.

When he returned, dressed more warmly, she spared him only a glance. He left without a word to her, only stopping long enough to listen to Davey's request for specific toys.

After he was gone, she enlisted Davey's help and they finished the task quickly. Wanting to lighten the oppressive mood that had filled the cabin, she decided to see if she still remembered how to handle a wood cookstove.

"I think I'll make a stew and some corn bread for when Mitch comes back. Want to help me?"

"You have to be careful, Mom. That stove can burn you. It's hot lots of places. Mitch makes me stay over by the counter." He dragged a chair over to the left of the stove and climbed up on it.

Perrie took his face in her hands and pressed a kiss to his hair. "I'm glad Mitch took such good care of you, but I'm better now. It would be best if you stayed with me and let him be by himself."

Blue eyes filled with rebellion. "But I like being with Mitch. He knows all kinds of things."

Perrie didn't let it show, but his words wounded. She and Davey had been all the other had for a long time now. It had been enough—until Mitch.

She would have to wean Davey away from this new fascination. Mitch would be gone from their lives all too soon. She would take it slowly, though.

As a gesture of peace, she asked, "Like what?"

He shrugged. "About animals and Indians and things." His eyes lit. "Did you know that the Indians thanked the animals they killed?" Tiny frown lines appeared. "I should have thanked my fish."

Perrie hid a smile and brushed back his hair. "You didn't know then."

"Mitch says it's not too late." A worried gaze met hers. "I don't know if I could shoot an animal."

Anger rose. "Did Mitch tell you that you must?"

"No. He didn't call me a baby like Dad did."

Perrie still burned at the memory of Simon calling Davey a coward when he'd wanted the three-year-old to try the high diving board on their indoor pool. She could still remember Davey's tears, the stark terror in his face as he stood on that high board. Despite her own fear, she had fought Simon—and paid later.

"Mitch said that it's a mat-matter of—" His forehead screwed up in concentration, then lightened. "Of balance. You should only take what you need, but sometimes there's too many animals of one kind and hunters have to help with the balance."

Why couldn't Simon have given his son the kindness of this stranger? "Do you understand what he's saying?"

"Sort of. He says that everything in nature is all hooked together." He concentrated again, then smiled. "Like a sweater that's knitted—that's what he said. Like the one you knitted me, Mom." Then worry crossed his face once more. "I don't see how animals and sweaters are very much alike. But I didn't tell Mitch 'cause he was looking so serious."

Perrie laughed. "We'll discuss that more later. For now, why don't you get me some of the little pieces of wood from the woodbin in the corner? Let's get this stove fired up."

"Okay!" He jumped off the chair and raced to the corner, blond hair bouncing.

Perrie studied the cookstove, making sure she remembered what to do. Woodbox on the left, water reservoir on the right. She'd already replaced the water she'd used to wash the clothes. The woodbox still held coals from breakfast. She'd use the small pieces of wood Mitch had cut just right to fit inside and raise the temperature in the stove.

Davey raced over, arms loaded with kindling. "This is enough to start, Mitch says."

Mitch says. Perrie shrugged away thoughts of how hard it would be to peel Davey away from his new idol. Maybe if she talked to Mitch, he would help her make it easier on Davey.

But that would mean discussing the plans she didn't yet have.

One step at a time. First, cook. Then rest. Then maybe she'd find her magic answer.

Carefully she fed the pieces of wood into the stove, then closed the lid. "Okay, let's see what we've got to work with."

"I know where things are. Mitch lets me help."

"You've always been a good helper."

Wrapping his arms around her waist, he hugged her tight. "I love you, Mom."

Tears pricked at her eyes. "I love you, too, sweetheart."

"Mitch will take care of us. We don't need Grandpa Cy. We can just stay here with Mitch. Okay, Mom?"

No, it's not okay. But she didn't say it. "Everything will work out, sweetheart. I promise." Silently she prayed for the answer to make that happen.

Perrie straightened and ruffled his hair. "Okay, young man. Let's get to cooking."

Mitch neared the cabin, flakes already beginning to fall. It looked like they were in for an early first storm—and a bad one, at that. He hoped he was wrong.

He'd slung one canvas bag over each shoulder and carried a suitcase in each hand. He hoped he'd correctly interpreted the toys Davey had requested, because making it down to the car again wouldn't be easy by tomorrow.

Stamping off his boots on the porch, Mitch set down the suitcases and opened the door.

And damn near stopped breathing.

If someone had slammed a fist between his eyes, it wouldn't have hit him any harder than the sight before him. He stepped inside and closed the door quietly.

She looked like a princess, even swathed in too-large gray fleece. Lying on the sofa, her arm curled around Davey, Perrie's back was turned to Mitch, her hair, for the first time, unbound and no longer wet.

Pure spun gold, it draped to the floor in a mass of waves that made him want to slide his fingers through as if he held silk in his hands.

His fingers itched to touch the shiny mass…to stroke the sweet line of her hip…to trail his touch from delicate shoulders to the small feet encased in his thick wool socks.

His clothes. Covering her curves.

Slipping the straps from his shoulders, he registered the rest of the changes. The cabin felt…cozy. Something cooking smelled great. The fire crackled welcome from the hearth, the room was warm. The woman would be warm.

Then Davey's eyes opened, wide and blue and smiling. Mitch tried to signal him to stay quiet and still so Perrie could sleep, but the warning came too late. Davey sat up.

With one hand above her head, Perrie arched like a cat, the sweatshirt sliding up to reveal more of her hips, more of the sweet curve of that bottom.

"Mitch!" Davey called out.

And the moment vanished. Perrie stiffened and sat up, turning to face him, her eyes wary. Davey scrambled to the floor and raced over to throw his arms around Mitch's waist.

Mitch couldn't help caressing the soft hair. Over the child's head, he and Perrie exchanged looks.

Hers was pure mother tigress. *Don't you hurt my child,* Perrie's gaze seemed to tell him.

His was more rebellious than it should have been. He had no business caring about someone else's boy. But he couldn't seem to quit.

Davey crowed. "Look, Mom, it's my bag. Yours, too." Then he registered the snow dusting Mitch's boots. "Is it snowing?"

"It's starting."

"Oh, boy! Wanna go make snow angels? We could have a snowball fight, too." One set of blue eyes danced with glee. The other set barked out a warning.

"Maybe later, sport. Right now, let's get your stuff inside."

"You carried more?"

Mitch opened the door and pulled the other two bags inside.

"My toys! Wow, Mitch, you're really strong— isn't he, Mom? Look at all he carried up here! Thanks, Mitch—wanna play with these?"

"Maybe in a little while." The walls closed in. He almost turned and went back outside. This felt too good. Too much like—

Home.

Don't be ridiculous. This is all an illusion. They'll be gone soon.

Very soon, if he had anything to say about it.

Davey immersed himself in greeting his toys like they were old friends he hadn't seen in years. Mitch resisted the urge to go back outside. Instead he busied himself removing his boots and coat, padding over to the fire in his stocking feet, ducking past the line of laundry.

Perrie approached but stayed on the other side of the line, speaking softly. "Thank you. It's very kind of you to do this. I didn't mean for you to carry so much."

He shrugged. "It wasn't hard."

"Is it getting bad outside?"

"Not yet, but it will be."

"I haven't spent much time up here except in the summers. Will it last long?"

"I haven't spent much time up here, either. I'm usually off guiding right now. But the first snow is unpredictable. Could come and go quick."

"But you don't think so."

He shook his head.

"I'm sorry. I'll do my best to keep Davey quiet and out of your way."

"Davey is not a problem." She was another matter.

She ducked her head, and golden hair spilled over her shoulder. He'd been right—it fell to her waist, a mass of honeyed silk. It was only too easy to imagine it spilling over her breasts, brushing his body. A golden curtain, sealing them off from the world.

He cursed silently and turned to face the fire.

Her voice was soft and hesitant. "I made a stew. I thought I'd do corn bread to go with it. Are you hungry?"

Ravenous. But they weren't talking about the same hunger.

Remember Cy. Remember what she did.

He whirled around. "Why wouldn't you take my call?"

Her eyes widened. "What call?"

"Don't play Miss Innocent. I called you when Cy was so sick I knew it was almost the end. You wouldn't even come to the phone."

"When was that?"

Fury shot through him. "You don't even remember?" He brushed past her hesitation. "In March. Some guy with a British accent answered the phone."

"Did you tell him who you were?" She got an odd look in her eyes, one he couldn't decipher.

"I didn't think it was anyone else's business. I told him it was an urgent family matter."

"What did he say?"

"He very politely told me that Miss Perrie had

no family and didn't like strangers calling her. He told me not to call again and hung up."

Perrie's glance darted everywhere but at him. "I never knew."

He snorted. "Or didn't care."

"I wasn't there then."

"Where were you?"

"Traveling." She wouldn't meet his eyes. She was lying. He'd almost swear it.

For a second he wanted to press her, to make her admit that she hadn't cared enough to keep in touch with the grandfather who had loved her.

But it wouldn't change anything. Cy would still be dead. Knowing wouldn't change how it had happened. He needed to get away from her, get a grip on his temper.

"I'll be—" Why was he explaining anything to her? "Never mind." Shaking his head, Mitch ducked under the line again and brushed past her, headed toward his bedroom.

"Mitch?"

He stopped in the doorway but didn't look back.

"Would you—" Her voice trembled slightly. "Shall I start the corn bread?"

He snorted and shook his head. "I can take care of myself, *Miss Perrie*. Don't dirty those lily-white hands on my account."

He heard the small intake of her breath and he felt a flicker of shame. But why?

He knew why. Because even if she was lying, she did care about Cy. He could hear it in her voice.

He wanted answers, but answers wouldn't undo anything.

It wasn't his business, anyway. The storm wouldn't last forever. This early in the fall, there would be a break between weather systems. And Perrie was getting stronger every day.

Soon she would be gone. Or he would.

It couldn't come a moment too soon.

Chapter Six

Perrie stared out the window, watching the world turn white. In the background, she faintly heard the sounds of Davey playing, but her mind whirled like the snowflakes that seemed to be coming more sideways than down in the ever-present Wyoming wind.

She could still see the accusation in Mitch's eyes, and it hurt. Lying wasn't in her nature, but she couldn't talk to him about Simon.

Could she?

What would happen if she did? Would this man, so dedicated to his solitude, want her to leave and take the threat away from his refuge?

Her sense of the man who was so careful with

her child was that he might not. He was strong. Hard. But curiously gentle with a boy who had not known the love of a father.

Perrie leaned her head against the cold glass, hoping to cool the boiling confusion in her brain.

Wasn't it true that, for the very reason of his kindness to Davey, she owed it to Mitch not to embroil him in the disaster her life had become?

And what about trust? He didn't trust her. Or like her.

But he might desire her. Those weren't gentle thoughts she sensed when his eyes raked her—and darkened.

Was she brave enough to risk exploring the attraction? Hadn't she had enough of darkness, of complicated men? Mitch didn't even know what his own brother looked like. How had that happened? Why would she rely upon a man who didn't keep in touch with his own family?

She couldn't. It was that simple. She could play roulette with her own life, but she couldn't take risks with Davey. He was all that was important. She'd made a mess of her life, but she wouldn't allow harm to come to her son. Mitch wouldn't harm him, she was sure of that. But she had no way to assure herself that he would welcome being embroiled in the tangle she'd made of her life with Simon.

You made your bed, Perrie. Now sleep in it. Alone.

For just a moment, she allowed her thoughts

rein…set herself free to imagine yielding to the temptation Mitch presented. Not just to sink into the comfort of his strength, but to give in to the draw of the smoldering sensuality he exuded with every breath.

He was a hard man, but beneath that shell she sensed more, something explosive. Deep within him something called, male to female, to something in her. She couldn't help wondering about how those strong, lean fingers would feel on her body, and the very wondering shocked her. Tantalized her. Never in her life had Perrie felt the pull of a man the way Mitch exerted a steady draw on her. Like the moon called to the tides, something deep within him made her want to respond.

But she was a mother first. She could not afford impulse.

Would not.

With effort, Perrie drew away from her fascination with the world outside the window and turned to her son.

"Davey?"

Davey looked up from his intense concentration on the figures he'd arranged on the rug.

"The ground is covered now. Want to go outside for a few minutes before we eat?"

His eyes glistened. "Yeah!"

"Okay. We have to bundle up like we would in Boston. There's not a lot of snow yet, but the wind is much stronger."

His joy brightened her own heart.

Concentrate on Davey. It's your only concern.

Davey raced out of the room, and Perrie followed behind him.

Mitch had heard them dressing, heard Davey's excitement and Perrie's whispered caution. But he had stayed in his bedroom, stretched out on his bed and staring at the ceiling.

Don't get involved. Caring brings pain.

Life had hammered that lesson into his brain with an emphasis he couldn't forget. He'd cared too much, felt too much. Lost control of his emotions—and a whole family had paid.

Where was Boone now? Davey's question haunted him. *Was* Boone his size? Two years younger, his brother had been almost his height the last time Mitch had seen him, when Boone was fourteen and Mitch two years older. Their father was a tall man, broad in the shoulders. Mitch had once thought Sam Gallagher the strongest man in the world.

Thoughts of his father stirred to life feelings that Mitch had thought he'd killed off years ago. The fury in Sam's face when Mitch had come home drunk for the umpteenth time. The worry in his mother's eyes. Her attempts to calm both him and Sam down.

To no avail.

Mitch remembered his father's words. *Get out of this house and don't ever come back. You're no son*

of mine. You're throwing your life away—for what?
You make me sick.

Mitch sat up quickly, rubbing both hands over
his face as if to scrub away what had happened
next. If only he'd kept his temper— If only his
mother hadn't followed him—

If only…if only… Two more useless words did
not exist in the English language.

His mother was dead. It was his fault. He
couldn't even blame Sam for banishing him forever
after that night.

He rose to pace the small room. Hadn't he
learned his lesson? The only safe path was not to
feel—anything. He'd begun to feel too much lately.

It had to stop.

He had to be careful, for the child's sake. Davey
gave his affection so easily, like it was as natural
as breathing. If Mitch had a son of his own, he'd
want him to be just like Davey.

But he would never have a son. He would live—
and die—alone.

And it was best that way.

Just ease away, he thought. Pull back slowly.
Don't get in any deeper. The boy was devoted to
his mother, and he had just latched on to Mitch
when he was the only adult awake. That was all.
Just that simple.

And if it bothered Mitch to lose the boy's growing devotion, well, he'd get over it. He'd gotten
over worse.

Mitch left his room, headed for the coffeepot. He

poured a cup and lifted the lid of the stew pot on the back of the stove.

Heaven. His mouth watered at the scent. Then he looked in the woodbox and saw that she knew how to handle a cookfire. She might be a pampered socialite forced into a few days of primitive living, but she obviously remembered what Cy had taught her.

And it smelled like she was a damn good cook. Mitch couldn't remember the last time someone else had cooked for him.

Just then, a shriek from outside drew him toward the window. Holding the full mug in his hand, Mitch watched Perrie and her son.

And smiled.

Davey pelted his mother with a small, mushy snowball that fell apart even before impact. Then he danced around, his arms lifted high in glee.

Perrie stood there, bundled in her own clothes, golden hair braided again, smiling like a teenage girl with no worries. Mitch hadn't realized, until he saw her now with all the caution smoothed from her face, just how tense she'd been since he'd met her. Around him, she was on edge. Even with Davey, she was always watchful, ever cognizant that she was a mother.

His mother had been like that. Good to him, good as any angel could have been. But firm. And always vigilant, wanting him safe.

Mitch closed his eyes, thinking about how he'd repaid her.

Don't let your anger win, Mitch, she'd said as she lay dying in his arms. He could still feel the cold trickle of the rain down his neck after he'd removed his hat to shield her. He could still see the trails of red washing out to pink on the gravel beside the road.

And even then, her only concern had been for him and for the others she'd loved. *Poor Mitch. Take care of Boone and Sam for me. I love you all,* she'd said.

Mitch watched Davey drop to the snow and fan his arms and legs, making a snow angel though the ground only held perhaps two inches of snow.

Perrie smiled and clapped, then answered Davey's pleas and lay down beside him, making her own snow angel.

The whole scene blurred as Mitch viewed it through the eyes of a boy who'd been loved...of a young man who'd laid love to waste.

He turned away from the window. He was older now. He'd learned to live without love a long time ago.

Perrie entered the living room with trepidation. With Davey now asleep, she was effectively alone with the glowering giant. Her bones ached with weariness, but she wasn't sleepy yet. Instead of sitting in the dark in the bedroom, she would brave the living room where Mitch sat before the fire.

He glanced up as she entered, then quickly back

to the piece of wood he was carving. "Davey's asleep?"

"Finally." She sank down on one corner of the sofa. The clothes had dried and been taken down before they'd eaten. She wished for the barrier between them again.

"It was a good meal. Thanks."

"Thank you for cleaning up." Such polite strangers, both of them, Perrie thought.

He shrugged. "Least I could do."

"Not hardly. Not after you hiked all that way to get our things."

He stared into the fire for long moments. "Cy taught you how to cook corn bread in the fireplace?"

She smiled, remembering. "The first time, I burned it to a crisp. Grandpa told me to rake some coals onto the hearth and set the pan there instead of on the fire, but I was in a hurry and thought the bread would cook faster with the coals where they were." She laughed faintly. "It did. Just not edibly."

A tiny smile quirked his lips. "My grandfather taught me to cook over a campfire. I've had my share of screwups."

"Was that who taught you to hunt? Your grandfather?" She held her breath, wondering if he'd answer.

The knife scraped against wood for a long time before he answered. "Yeah. He taught me to fish when I was about Davey's size."

"Did you always like it?"

He nodded. "A lot more than ranch work."

So he'd grown up on a ranch. She waited, hoping he'd tell her more, but he didn't.

She needed to thank him for what he'd done. "Davey told me what you said about thanking his fish."

She saw his shoulders stiffen and she rushed to explain. "Thank you for not making him feel foolish that he's tenderhearted about animals. His father—" How could she explain without telling too much? "His father wasn't so thoughtful."

The dark head turned in her direction. "I wasn't so tough myself at his age. I liked fishing, but I had my squeamish moments. I don't trust anyone who kills without remorse." Brown eyes softened. "What did his father say?"

She shrugged. "It wasn't about hunting or fishing. When Davey was three, his father thought he should try the high diving board." Anger rose again, tightening her throat. "He called Davey a coward because he was afraid."

Mitch swore under his breath. "His father was a fool. That boy has the heart of a lion. He was ready to take me on to protect you."

Perrie met his gaze, seeing the fierce pride glow. Pride. For her son.

Why couldn't Simon have been like that?

Useless thoughts. "He's got his stubborn streak, but he has a good heart." She smiled. "Protecting me, huh? How sweet."

"Not a lot of five-year-olds would make their way through an unfamiliar forest to get help. He was scared to death of me, but he didn't give an inch. Stood over you like a guard dog." Mitch shook his head once. "Hell of a kid."

The way he looked at her, the questions in his eyes, made her wish she could explain their lives.

But as she searched for answers, he saved her the choice, rising to his feet. "Well, I'm turning in. It's been a long day."

"Mitch—" She had to get this one thing straight. "Davey's getting so attached to you. I—" How did she say this?

Again he saved her the trouble.

"It won't last. He just latched on to me because you were sick. Once the storm has let up, I'll make myself scarce until you're well enough to go."

But she was watching him as he said it, and despite his words, she could see a shadow cross his face.

For a moment, she thought she saw hunger in those dark eyes.

The hunger of a man too long alone.

She'd never met a man more solitary in her life. But hearing the fondness in his voice when he spoke of his grandfather...seeing his eyes when he spoke of her son...Perrie had to wonder, yet again, what had made this man close himself off from love.

She felt an urge to comfort him, to bring him

closer to the fire, like a dark wolf who roamed the perimeter of a campsite, starving to death.

But that was foolish in the extreme. He wouldn't thank her for her sympathy, she knew instinctively. He was a grown man, a strong man who had made it through life without her help. Davey must be her only concern.

So she merely nodded at him and closed off the part of her heart open to his pain.

"Thank you." *And I'm sorry. More sorry than I can say.*

Mitch lay in his bed and listened to Perrie moving around the cabin, wishing she'd just go to bed and let him be. Quit playing with his mind.

But his mind didn't want to quit playing with her.

She wasn't the china doll he'd first thought. Oh, she looked like one, all right, all big blue eyes, creamy skin and rosy lips. And that hair. His fingers still itched to tangle themselves in it, to stroke from scalp to tips, letting the waves shift against his skin like ribbons of silk. The one sight he'd had of it unbound made him understand why the sight used to be reserved for a woman's husband. He understood why hair was called a woman's crowning glory.

He wanted to loose it from its braid, separate the heavy skeins with his fingers. Feel it brush over his body with languid, drifting strokes. For a bittersweet moment, he wished that she was someone else—and that he was. That they could meet as strangers. Nothing between them but the night and the wanting.

He turned over with a groan, his body hard and aching.

Damn this storm.

He punched the pillow again and shifted against the sheets. Squeezing his eyes shut, he searched for sleep. But sleep taunted him like a scornful lover.

Who was Perrie Matheson, really? Was she the callous socialite who hadn't cared enough to come when her only kin needed her? Mitch wasn't sure what a socialite should look like, but Perrie didn't fit any description he could imagine. Her car was several years old and nondescript. Her slender fingers sported no jewels, her nails were short and unpainted. The only clothes she'd worn so far had seen better days.

And she was stronger than she looked. Still physically weak from her illness, she'd put in a full day's labor, anyway. Hadn't considered herself too good to wash his socks. Had cooked a damn good meal on a cantankerous stove.

There was more to her than one would think, just looking at her small frame. But she was lying to him—he knew it. Why? With every day that passed, Mitch found himself more curious, yet as someone with plenty of his own secrets to hide, he'd made it a religion not to pry into the lives of others.

Live and let live, had been his motto. Don't get involved. Pack light and move fast.

And silence is golden.

She had a right to her secrets. And he didn't need the hassles. A few more days, that's all he had to survive.

A few more days of watching her…and wondering.

Of wanting to touch.

Of seeing the world through Davey's eyes, feeling the magic of the boy's innocent wonder.

Of seeing a mirage that mocked a longing he'd thought long ago drained from his very bones. The way the woman and the boy had moved into a stark cabin—

And made it feel treacherously like what he remembered of home.

Mitch bolted up in the bed and scrabbled for a match in the moonlight. He lit the kerosene lamp and reached for a book—any book—to make the hours pass until dawn.

In the faint morning light, Perrie worked as silently as possible to build up the fire. She should have left the bedroom door open last night to draw in some of the heat, but she'd wanted distance. Waking up to a frigid room had been a real jolt to the system. She'd covered Davey with her own blankets and left the door open.

Mitch's door was closed, too. It was the first time she'd ever awakened before him. She thought about opening his door at least a crack but reminded herself that he was a grown man—and a very private one, at that.

In a few minutes more, she had the coffeepot bubbling on top of the stove, and she was able to remove some of the clothing she'd worn for her trip outside.

The world was a white wonderland. That was the good news.

It was still snowing. That was the bad. This cabin was too small to live in a state of armed warfare with anyone. She and Mitch would have to come to some accommodation if they were to survive with their sanity intact.

Last night they'd had an actual conversation, without rancor. The contempt that had filled his eyes since the first day had been replaced by a wary politeness. Maybe there was hope that they could come to some sort of accord, some way to make do until the snow stopped.

She turned at the sound of footsteps, to see Mitch's head buried beneath the shirt he was shrugging on. For the briefest of instants, she saw his bare chest, ridged with muscle and covered with dark whorls of hair tapering down to a fine line bisecting his flat belly.

Then the dark blue fleece shirt came down to cover it.

Wait, she wanted to say. *Let me see that again.*

Perrie could barely stifle a gasp at her own thoughts. She'd never felt an urge like that before. Heat blossomed in her center and spread to her face.

Mitch's startled gaze met hers. For an unguarded second, his eyes took on a glow that burned right into her. Caught like prey in the heat of his eyes, she found herself unable to look away.

Then his shutters slammed closed again. She quickly averted her eyes, but she was so rattled that she brushed one hand against the stove, jerking back reflexively, sucking in a breath at the stab of pain.

"Are you okay?"

She whirled at the sound of his voice right behind her and she stumbled backward.

Strong arms shot out to pull her away from the stove.

And into the solid wall of his chest.

She wanted to lean into him, to wrap her arms around his waist and hold tight. She'd never felt as safe in her life as she did with Mitch around.

But deep within her, the woman scented danger. This man was all male. Too male for someone like her.

She pushed against his chest, stepping carefully away from temptation. One glance at his face showed her a jaw gone rock hard, eyes turned cold.

"Let me see your hand," he ordered, reaching for her after a hesitation that showed his unwillingness to touch her any more than he must.

She jerked her hand back. "It's fine—I just—" she stammered. "I made coffee—"

"Don't be foolish," he growled, reaching for her hand again. "You can't be careless with wounds up here. Medical help is too far away." He turned her palm upward, then to the side. Then he grabbed a cup from the dish rack and moved to the door, opening it and scooping up snow. He returned and shoved it toward her. ''Hold the spot against this for a few minutes.''

Then he walked away, shrugging on his coat and knit cap and heading outside, leaving Perrie staring after him.

So much for the truce. But armed dislike might be safer than that quick riot of feelings he'd provoked. Her mind drifted back to that brief, electric glimpse of skin. He had the muscles of a working man, not the pretty-boy bulk built in gyms. He was big. Powerful. And he made something deep inside her ache.

She'd had a crush or two when she was younger—all those towns where her mother drifted meant that she'd been exposed to lots of boys in lots of different schools. But the increasing stares from her mother's boyfriends had kept her wary of the male of the species. And the last one—well, he'd scared her enough for her to leave for good.

And after that she'd been too busy to worry about boyfriends of her own. All her time and efforts had been focused on survival, on working and finishing school and getting that first plum secretarial job that would lead her away from her mother's life.

Fate had intervened, giving her that job at Matheson Industries, and she'd attracted Simon's attention. He'd seemed worlds away from the squalor of her youth, like he could lift her up into a life that was pristine and orderly, free of any remnant of the life she'd escaped. But she'd discovered darkness in his world, too.

Perrie had never felt like this before. Too warm, achy and restless in a way that made no sense.

But if this were desire, Mitch wouldn't welcome it. Or share it. Simon had given her ample evidence that she wasn't the kind of woman who could satisfy a man. She was no good at passion.

But still something called to her, made her wonder, made her wish, just a little. Foolish or not.

No harm in wondering, right? All too soon, she and Davey would be gone.

Perrie removed her hand and studied the faint red streak, assuring herself that it was minor. Then she looked out the window again, smiling wistfully at her thoughts. For one bittersweet moment she remembered how his body had felt against hers, how his dark eyes had sparked.

Suddenly Perrie was sick to death of being careful. Tired of playing it safe, of being afraid of every shadow, every single misstep.

She wouldn't do anything about how Mitch made her feel—couldn't, because they must go soon. But that didn't mean she couldn't imagine how it would be, if he didn't want her gone—and she didn't have to leave. If they were alone here, just the two of them, no past to come between them, no future to decide.

She didn't have to tell anyone, least of all Mitch. But in her own private thoughts she could spin a new kind of story. One in which two bodies, one dark and one fair, intertwined. One in which whatever this feeling was that Mitch stirred could be explored.

Where maybe, just maybe, she could coax the lone wolf to the fire, even for a minute.

Then she heard the front door opening and quickly fled to the room she shared with Davey.

Chapter Seven

"I can't do this." Davey sighed, crumpling the length of soft rope in his hand.

Perrie started to soothe him, but Mitch spoke up first.

"I thought the same thing when I was learning." He smiled at her son as he'd never smiled at her. "Come here." He set down the piece of wood he was whittling and scooted forward on his chair, patting his thigh. "Come stand right here."

He settled Davey in front of him, reaching around her son's body. "Let me hold these ends for you again."

Patiently he instructed Davey through the steps of tying a square knot once more, his deep voice gentle and calm, no matter how Davey's fingers fumbled.

Perrie watched her child's intense concentration, watched the big hands work with the tiny ones as the fire lit the two of them with a golden glow.

And for a moment she felt the lash of regret. Davey should have had this all his life. Should have been granted a father who would care for him, guide him, show him how to be a man like—

A man like Mitch.

She jerked her gaze away from them, shocked to her marrow at the direction of her thoughts.

Mitch wasn't a father, didn't pretend to be one. Or to want to.

He was a rolling stone, gathering no moss.

He was a difficult man, hard and cynical. He had no interest in the family he had, much less in acquiring a new one.

And she—did she want another man in her life? A man to restrict her, to shove her into his own definition of who she should be? To walk away from Davey when he was too much trouble?

No. Absolutely not. She and Davey were enough for each other. It was that simple. She would care for Davey until he was grown, and then—

What would her life be, once Davey was gone? For that was the way of nature—babies grew up and left the nest. She would be alone.

Alone, as she'd been so often in her life. Her mother hadn't been interested in motherhood at all.

She'd wanted laughter and good times and raucous fun.

Only with Grandpa Cy, only in these mountains, had she found peace. Only here had she felt like she'd belonged.

"Look, Mom! Look what I did!" Davey rushed to her side to show her the knot he'd made with Mitch's help.

Over her child's blond head, she met Mitch's gaze. *Thank you,* she wanted to say. Hoped she was saying, with her eyes.

Thank you for caring more than his own father ever did.

"This is wonderful," she responded. "You did such a good job." She drew Davey close, breathing in that little-boy smell. "I'm very proud of you."

And then she lifted her gaze again, capturing in Mitch's eyes a naked longing that hurt her to her soul.

Her throat thickened with tears she dared not shed. She held his gaze, measure for measure, refusing to look away.

Dark eyes studied her own for long moments, within them a maelstrom of need and confusion...and a loneliness so deep that her heart ached.

For that span of time, she felt closer to him than she'd felt to anyone but Davey in years. It made no sense, given that he had never uttered a word to make her think he wanted more than he had.

Caught in the grasp of his powerful spirit, Perrie could barely resist the sigh that threatened. A sigh that reached out to this solitary man. Part wish to comfort him, part longing for a safe harbor of her own.

When Davey spoke, she felt jarred to her bones.

"Tell me more about Ermengilda, Mom," he pleaded.

Perrie snapped her gaze away from Mitch's. She could barely remember her own name, much less Ermengilda's story. "Oh, sweetie, I don't think Mitch wants to hear that."

"Sure he does—" Davey turned. "Don't you, Mitch? I told you my mom makes up cool stories. This one's about a princess who's a fish."

When Mitch's amused look met hers, Perrie felt her cheeks warm.

"Ermengilda?" Mitch asked.

"Yeah," Davey laughed. Then he sobered. "But don't kid Mom about it." His voice dropped to a whisper. "She likes it."

Mitch's brown eyes lightened to amber. His mouth quirked at the corners when he looked at her.

She was beginning to wish she were anywhere but here. "I haven't thought much about her lately," she said weakly.

Davey's big blue eyes turned downcast. "Aw, Mom, couldn't you try, just a little?" he wheedled.

She glanced at Mitch, who seemed to be enjoying her discomfort. For a moment, she thought about how good that harsh face looked, lit with the seeds of laughter.

She owed him this, at the very least, for all he'd

done for them. Mitch had had little laughter in his life, she was almost certain.

So she swallowed hard and tried to ignore the steady glow of those dark eyes as she searched for the thread of her story.

"So where were we?" she asked Davey.

He climbed up on her lap, a smug smile on his face. "Ermie was laughing when that dumb boy was tickling her."

She poked him gently in the ribs. "Princess Ermengilda, young man. And the prince isn't dumb."

"But he has blue eyes, right? Just like mine?"

She smiled. "Just like yours."

"And we get to have a sword fight?"

Perrie heard Mitch's chuckle and glanced up to see him shaking his head. "What is it about boys and fighting?" she asked.

His face sobered. "Men protect. That's part of who we are, since time began." A darkness crossed his face, a stab of pain that made her want to soothe, to seek out his sorrow.

Had he failed to protect someone? Was that the sadness that filled him?

"Mom?" Davey wiggled in her lap. "So what's next?"

Perrie jerked her gaze away from the man who was such an enigma. Drawing a deep breath, she grasped for the threads of the story.

"When we left them, Ermengilda was laughing so hard she couldn't swim away. The Prince of the Pretty People was tickling her belly, and she felt all her bones turn to jelly. The next thing she knew, she was way up in the air, gasping for breath—

"Prince of the Pretty People—eck." Davey turned to Mitch and rolled his eyes. "Men can't be pretty, can they, Mitch?"

"It was never a goal of mine."

He wasn't pretty, no. But he had a hard, dark beauty of his own. Compelling...haunting...his face was one she would never forget.

"Then what, Mom?" Davey asked.

Mitch turned back to his whittling, and Perrie grasped at scattered thoughts.

"The prince was looking at her very closely. Ermengilda was a little nervous at first, but she was sure he didn't mean to harm her. So she spoke to him first."

"Fish can talk, too?"

"In my story they can."

Davey shrugged and settled against her chest. "So what did she say?"

"She said, 'If you'll tell me you love me, I'll become a beautiful princess and we can marry.'"

"What did the prince do?"

"He laughed and almost dropped her." Perrie wasn't sure which rewarded her most—Davey's broad smile...or Mitch's soft chuckle.

She went on. "When she recovered her wits, she looked him straight in the eye and said, 'You don't believe me, do you?'

"'You're just a fish,' he said. 'Besides, I don't want to marry anyone.'

"'But you have to,' she cried out. 'Otherwise, I can't become The True Princess.'

"'What's a true princess?'

"'*The* True Princess. The one who inherits the kingdom and tells everyone what to do and everyone lives happily ever after.'

"The prince snorted. 'I wouldn't live happily, if you were telling me what to do all the time.'"

Davey giggled. Mitch's mouth curved at the corners. Perrie wanted to be clever and witty and keep them both smiling, but she had no idea where this story was going.

"But just then, Ermengilda couldn't say any more. She couldn't breathe except in gasps.

"'What's wrong?' the prince asked.

"'Can't—' She tried her hardest to speak. When nothing else would come out, she tried to flap her gills on his palm in Morse code so he'd understand that she needed to get back into the water."

"What's Morse code?" Davey asked.

Mitch grinned as though he was very familiar with Davey's penchant for questions.

Perrie wished he would face her so she could see those dark, haunted eyes lighten. She stirred herself to answer. "It's a system of long and short taps that translate into letters."

"Do you know it, Mom?

She had to shake her head. "Sorry."

"I bet Mitch does, right?"

He did look over then, and she caught her breath

at the fondness she saw in his gaze. "Yeah." He nodded. "I do."

"Will you teach me?"

A faint shadow crossed his face, and she knew what he must be thinking. They wouldn't be together long enough for that.

Honesty warred with affection in his expression. He might not want her here, but he had a hard time resisting Davey.

"I'll show you what I can," he offered.

That was enough for her son, who settled back against her. But Mitch's look at her wasn't so easy for her to dismiss. She couldn't decide how much was apology, how much resentment. Things would be much simpler for both of them if Davey weren't part of the equation.

"Did he get it, Mom? The Morse code? And how long until the sword fight?"

Humor flickered in Mitch's dark gaze once more. Perrie had to smile back, shaking her head.

"I was thinking of kisses next."

"Eck," Davey protested. "Leave them out."

"But princes and princesses have to kiss," she teased, knowing it would drive him up the wall. She leaned down and nuzzled him, making loud smacking kiss noises against his cheek.

"Stop, M-Mom," he stammered between raucous giggles, squirming in her lap until he'd slipped down.

He turned to Mitch. "Guys don't really like to

kiss, right?'' His voice clearly expressed his opinion.

Mitch flicked a quick glance at Perrie, his dark eyes unreadable as they scanned her face. But when his look lingered on her mouth, Perrie's breath tightened in her chest. Their gazes held—until he tore his away.

He shrugged. ''Kissing is natural between men and women.''

''Do you want to kiss Mom, now that you're not mad at her?''

''Davey!'' Perrie gasped.

Mitch stiffened. ''Your mom and I aren't—it's not like that.'' He stared at the floor, then turned to her son, while studiously avoiding looking at her. ''A man can't just kiss a woman because he's not mad at her. There's more to it.''

''Like what?'' Davey asked.

If Perrie weren't so uncomfortable herself, she might be tempted to laugh at Mitch's expression. He looked like he wished he were anyplace but here.

She knew the feeling. ''That's enough, Davey. It's time for you to go to bed now.''

His voice turned to wheedling. ''Why? I don't have anywhere to go tomorrow. We're just gonna be stuck inside here again.''

''Don't argue with your mother,'' Mitch said.

Perrie wanted to bristle that he'd given her son orders, but she observed the same phenomenon she'd seen before. When Mitch gave orders, Davey never argued.

"Okay." Meek as a lamb, Davey turned toward the bedroom. Just before he reached the doorway, he whirled back and raced across to throw his arms around Mitch.

Mitch quickly set the knife away from him, looking like he'd been poleaxed.

"Good night, Mitch." Davey's small hands tightened on those very broad shoulders.

Mitch shot her a troubled glance. Then he bent his head and wrapped his own arms around her child, his thick dark lashes sweeping down, hiding his eyes for a brief second. His voice seemed rusty as he answered, "Good night." He pulled back awkwardly. "Sleep well."

"Sweet dreams. That's what my mom says," Davey offered. Then he bent past Mitch's arm. "What's that? Is that a bear?"

Mitch shrugged. "Yeah."

"Wow, Mom. You should see this. Look, it's exactly like a bear."

Still caught up in the whirlwind of her own confusion, Perrie didn't want to get any nearer.

"I—" Mitch actually looked shy now. "If you like it, you could have it."

"Me?" Davey's eyes widened. "Can I have it now?" He turned back to her. "Can I have it, Mom?"

"Sweetie, I don't think—" She was about to explain that he shouldn't make Mitch feel like he had to give it to him, when Mitch looked at her, his face guarded again.

"It's not much. I just thought maybe—" He looked away, his jaw hardening.

She'd handled this wrong. He was a proud man, and unaccustomed to being with people. "I didn't mean that. I just didn't want you to feel like you had to give it to him because he begged."

Mitch shot her a glare. "He didn't beg. I offered." His shoulders shrugged. "I was making it for him, anyway."

"You were? For me?" Davey leapt and clapped his hands. "Can I sleep with it?"

The hard face softened slightly. Perrie almost thought she saw his cheeks color, though it could have been the fire's glow.

"I'm not quite finished carving, and it needs to be sanded."

"Oh." Davey's voice turned small. He lifted his gaze, his expression crafty. "I could just watch it for you tonight, until you're ready to work on it some more."

Then she heard a sound she never expected to hear: Mitch's laughter. Rusty, like it had fallen into disrepair. But a laugh, for all its brevity and disuse.

A large hand ruffled her son's tousled hair. "Good idea. You keep him warm tonight, and I'll work on him more later."

"All right!" Davey picked up the bear, cradling it carefully in his hands for a few slow, measured steps. Then the real Davey returned as he raced across the floor, juggling it in his fingers. "Look, Mom! Mitch made this for me."

Perrie glanced at the wooden figure, just the right size to fit in Davey's hand. For a moment, her heart actually hurt in the rush of sorrow for all Davey deserved and had never had. For the hard, lonely man who had a soft spot for her son.

For how it had felt here tonight, like all her dreams of what family life should be. Quiet, simple moments filled with affection. Not between her and Mitch, of course. But for this span of hours, Davey had had a sample of the way she'd always believed a child deserved to be raised. Under the protection of a strong, caring man, wrapped in a mother's love.

But it was only an illusion. Fighting past too many feelings, Perrie clenched her hands and peered down into Davey's hands.

It was exquisite.

She glanced up in surprise. "You're very talented."

Mitch shrugged. "Just something to pass the time."

"Where did you learn to do this?"

"My grandfather taught me. And my dad used to do it in the evenings when the family gathered. He wasn't much for sitting still, but we liked to hear my mother read stories." Then he fell silent, his face darkening with memories that would probably explain a lot of who he was.

She wanted to ask. It was the deepest glimpse yet, a tiny fragment of who he was, where he'd been. But she could already see him drawing away into himself. And she didn't want him asking her questions, either.

She gave him an out. "You've obviously practiced," she remarked. "It's beautiful." She turned to her son. "Be very careful with it, Davey."

"I will." Then he darted across the floor again, clutching the bear tightly while he embraced Mitch once more. "Thanks, Mitch."

The big man patted his back, nodding but saying nothing.

Perrie wished she could see the eyes looking fixedly into the fire.

Slowly Mitch drew away and averted his gaze.

She held out her hand to her child. "Okay. Time for bed now."

Davey didn't even murmur a protest. At the doorway he stopped and turned. "Mitch?"

The dark head turned, his eyes unreadable. "What?"

"I'll take good care of him."

Mitch's jaw flexed. "I know you will." Then he turned back to the fire, and she could almost see him drawing within himself again.

For the fortieth time since they'd left the room, Mitch fought the urge to grab his coat and head outside, regardless of the weather.

He wasn't made for this, staying so long in one place. He was used to being active, to the constant vigilance required to lead others into the wilderness, to the attention to detail such trips required.

For a while tonight he'd felt almost peaceful. Hands busy carving, he'd listened to the gentle play between Perrie and her child, to the soft laughter, the ease between them. For a while, he'd felt something inside him unfurl, something that had been twisted tight for so long that he'd quit noticing its tension.

Now he felt—hell, what *did* he feel? Itchy... uneasy. Angry.

Touched. Warmed by the boy's delight.

But crowded. Unable to figure out how this could end right, without hurting Davey.

He shoved to his feet, cursing ripely. He had no business caring about the boy. He lived alone, would die alone. The child would leave, would grow up, would forget all about these days in the mountains. Would forget him, too.

And the knowledge sank like a stone into the deep empty well inside him. He'd been forgotten before.

Where was his brother now? Did Boone ever think about him? Had his father ever softened?

No reason why Sam should. And no sense thinking about a life that was gone forever.

It was *them*, the woman and the child—they made him wonder. Made him remember. He would be fine when they left.

If the damn snow would ever stop. Perrie wasn't too far from being ready to travel.

And Mitch was more than ready for her to go.

A book. He would read until sleep claimed him. Mitch shoved away from his study of the fire, turning toward the door—

Just as she stepped into the room.

They both stopped in their tracks, going perfectly still. Blue eyes studied him, and saw too much.

They each spoke at once.

"You were very kind to—"

"Don't—"

The long braid shifted across the shoulder of her pale yellow sweater, and suddenly all he could see was the fall of blond silk that haunted his dreams.

His voice too harsh, he gestured to her. "Ladies first."

She flipped the braid over her back and straightened, drawing a deep breath. Her fingers tightened around one another. "I hope Davey didn't impose on you. He thinks that bear is wonderful, but if you meant to keep it—"

"I don't say things I don't mean. I made it for him."

Her eyes filled with warmth. "He's already very attached to it." A faint smile flitted across her lips. "I hope you can get it back to do whatever's left. He tends to get possessive of things he loves. He doesn't have—" She glanced away. "His life hasn't been all that I'd planned."

Mitch saw the shadow descend over her face, and he wanted to bring back the light that had sparkled while she spun her tale.

"That's some story you're telling him. You do that often?"

Her gaze lifted to his, studying him to see what he meant. Then her dark lashes swept down, color dusting her cheeks. For the first time, he noticed that faint golden freckles sprinkled her nose. That her hair had strands of red and brown tossed in with the honey.

That one step would bring him close enough to touch.

Close enough to kiss.

The fire crackled, and it sounded like gunshots, so intense was his focus on her. He took one quick step back.

Her lashes swept upward, a tiny smile playing around her lips. Oblivious to his thoughts, she looked to the side while she explained. "I guess I've always had quite an imagination. I used to tell Grandpa stories at night, and he seemed to enjoy them. He even told me I should write them down, but I—" She shrugged. "I just do them for my own enjoyment. Just simple stories."

"A princess trout? Not so simple. And Davey sure likes it."

Her smile was fond. "I haven't been able to give him everything I'd hoped, but the stories are something I can give him anytime. Anyplace." For a moment, she looked sad. Weary.

He wanted to ask why. Make her tell him what was wrong. Even if it was none of his concern.

Then she glanced up. "Sometimes he makes up

his own stories to tell me.'' This time her smile was broad. ''His tend toward epic battles, with lots of bams and pows.''

He was caught in the warmth of her smile. ''Not much kissing.''

She laughed then, shaking her head. ''Never.''

Then there it was, bursting into life between them again. Something he couldn't name—didn't want to. Something rich and dark and tempting—but with a bite to it, a hint of spice.

Her pupils went wide, turning blue into navy, her nostrils flaring slightly as if she caught the scent, too, of whatever it was that swirled thick as wood smoke between them. To his surprise, she didn't move away, though her body held the wariness of a doe poised for flight.

One step—that's all it would take to have them body to body, mouth touching mouth. He could taste that fragile skin, lap up the ruby sweetness inside. He could bare her flesh once more, but this time slowly...privately...savoring every inch that he'd struggled not to notice before.

And she'd let him. He could feel it pouring over him, the languid warmth of her desire. She might regret it later—absolutely would—but she wanted him now.

As he wanted her.

He should do it—take that step, reach out and grasp what he wanted. Forget the questions, forget that it was temporary, only a shadow of what would fill this damned hunger of the heart.

He would have, for however long it lasted, the blessed surcease of oblivion that only this woman's warm, willing body could provide. He wouldn't hurt her; he would make it good for her, no matter how sharp the edges of his wanting. And she wasn't as fragile as she looked. Though she was small, she was strong in spirit.

And that, of course, was why he wouldn't. Why he would leave her alone.

Because her valor humbled him. She was strong enough to be gentle, brave enough to eschew pity. Something weighed heavily on her, but she asked no quarter, had not wanted to be treated like porcelain, had pitched in and done more than she should.

So when Perrie's lids drifted downward and she swayed toward him the slightest inch, Mitch did what he should, instead of what he wanted.

He walked away.

To save them all.

Chapter Eight

When Perrie awoke, the first thing on her mind was the brilliant sunshine. The second was the fool she'd made of herself last night.

Stifling a groan, she rolled over and curled on her side, wanting to pull the covers over her head and stay there forever.

Fool. Idiot. What were you thinking?

She could have sworn Mitch wanted to kiss her. But maybe what she sensed was only how badly she wanted to kiss him. It had taken her hours to fall asleep, replaying that scene in her mind—remembering that they'd gone beyond his contempt, beyond stiff politeness, and finally, actually had had a conversation that was almost friendly.

And that somewhere, all of that had changed. Somehow the air had thickened with almost palpable emotion, so charged that she'd succumbed to its seductive lure, let herself want.

He'd been so close that she could almost feel him, could smell that scent that was only Mitch— part forest, part wood smoke...all powerfully male.

He'd made her feel safe before, but this was totally different. She wanted to clutch at those sinewy arms, slide her fingers into that dark, tousled hair, feel the connection of her body against the solid length of his.

And she'd swear he'd felt it, too, in that charged moment when time had seemed to stand still.

But when she'd closed her eyes, unable to look at his dark beauty any longer without betraying herself—

He'd said good-night and walked away without a backward glance.

What did you expect, Perrie? Simon told you you're no good at this. You're not a passionate woman, that's all there is to it. There's something missing in you.

But for one tantalizing instant, she'd thought it might be different with Mitch.

She rolled over again, burrowing deeper under the covers. She'd never be able to face him again. She squeezed her eyes shut and shook her head. Then she drew a deep, steadying breath and threw back the covers, leaping from the bed.

She had to face him, whether she wanted to or

not. She'd done lots of things in her life that had seemed impossible at first. Facing Mitch would be nothing compared to escaping Simon.

Perrie's eyes widened as she realized that she hadn't thought of Simon in over a day. Not one thought. Not a whisper of worry.

It was a record. Simon had dominated her life for years now. *Please, God, let this last. Don't let him find us.*

The butter-gold bars of sunshine sprouted the seeds of hope in her heart. Perrie felt the first stirrings of optimism that she would figure it all out, would find a path for Davey and herself, even if it meant leaving this place.

Even if it meant facing Mitch. Even asking him where they stood, regarding the cabin.

He wasn't inside, she was almost sure. Somehow, the cabin felt different when he was there. Once she would have said it felt crowded, but now it felt empty when he was gone. But that wasn't her concern. Either he would go or they would—that was the certain end.

And knowing that she would handle it, whatever came, renewed her strength. She felt almost like her old self again—not just before her illness, but like the girl who had once thought she could control her fate.

The girl had been wrong, but there were seeds of her that Perrie could use. She could work hard, she could learn, she could make herself and Davey a good life.

So when Davey's eyes popped open, she greeted him with a smile. "Morning, sleepyhead. Rise and shine."

He glanced at the window. "Wow, sunshine! Can we go outside today? Can we take a walk and look around, so I can show you some cool places Mitch showed me?"

Perrie nodded. "I think a walk sounds just great."

"Slow down, Davey," Perrie called out. Mitch still had not appeared by lunchtime, so she'd fixed them lunch and left the stew warming on the back of the woodstove.

Her steps slowed as she reached the small clearing.

Davey darted here and there, all the energy of the two days before exploding from his small frame after being released from the cabin's boundaries. "Look, Mom, I see tracks over there—"

Perrie couldn't answer. Before her stood the grandfather spruce Grandpa Cy had called the Old Man of the Mountain.

You know the grandfather spruce? ...I scattered his ashes there.

Perrie's hands clasped between her breasts, her vision blurred by her tears.

"Mom, come—" Davey's voice turned worried. "What's wrong?"

She could barely hear him, lost in a thousand memories of the gruff old man who'd been her foundation. Over all the years her mother had dragged her from place to place, boyfriend to boyfriend, the only anchor in Perrie's world had been Cy Blackburn.

You didn't care enough…too bad you broke his heart.

She dropped to her knees, doubled over by the pain.

I'm so sorry, Grandpa. I should have been here. If only I'd known—

''Mom?'' Davey was standing close now, close enough to touch. ''What's the matter?''

She shook her head and opened her arms, enfolding him in her embrace and rocking him from side to side while tears rolled down her cheeks.

Davey hugged her once, tightly, then pulled back. ''You're sad?''

She nodded, sliding first one palm and then the other across her damp face. ''I'll be all right.''

''Is it Grandpa Cy? Is that why you're sad?''

Perrie tried for a smile, then pulled Davey down on her lap, mindless of the snow under her knees. ''He would have loved you so much.''

''That's what Mitch said.''

She blinked at that, surprised at Mitch's generosity. He would never forgive her, but she would never forgive herself, either. She should have been in touch the first instant she was away from Simon. She should have sensed, somehow, that Grandpa needed her. Should have felt in her bones that something was wrong with the most important man in her life.

Not for the first time, Perrie felt the rage of shame for what she'd gotten herself into, for being a blind, naïve fool, for letting Simon dominate her for so long.

"Maybe you could talk to Grandpa Cy like Mitch told me I could still thank my fish. It might not be too late."

From the mouths of babes. Feeling an odd spurt of hope, she set Davey on his feet, then rose herself and held out her hand. "I think you're right. Let's give it a try."

Hand in hand, they crossed the white powder. The wind blew through the trees, keening a faint moan that could be a dirge. "Grandpa Cy loved these mountains," she told Davey. "He never tired of their changing seasons, of the different faces they showed, day to day, and year to year. He called this big tree the Old Man of the Mountain. He said that if I would listen closely, I'd hear the stories this tree could tell."

"Did you ever listen?"

Perrie had to smile. "I tried, but I was never very good at sitting still."

Davey giggled at that. "Wiggle worm. Just like you call me."

She squeezed his hand and nodded, then looked out toward the eastern sky. "Old Man of the Mountain, please tell my grandfather that I love him. And that I'm sorry, so sorry. I miss him so much."

When Davey's small hand squeezed hers and he leaned against her, the tears came again. "Here's my son Davey, Grandpa. You'd be so proud of him." Her throat clogged.

But Davey took over for her. "Mitch is taking good care of us, Grandpa Cy. He made me this bear." Holding his hand out toward the tree, Davey displayed the wooden friend who hadn't left his side once today. His voice dropped a little. "I think Mitch misses you a lot."

Perrie sank to the ground and crossed her arms over her stomach, doubling over and rocking her body, trying to find comfort. Desperately she grasped for steady ground. She shouldn't have come here with Davey. Her grief hurt too much, was too raw for a child.

With the last vestiges of her will, Perrie clenched her fists and pulled herself together, forcing herself to sit up straight, thinking of what Grandpa had once said. *You're the strong one, Perrie. You have no father, and your mother, well, she's one of the lost souls. But you, you're a little speck of flesh, but there's strength in you like in these rugged old mountains. Nothing life can hand you that you can't take. I wish I could keep you here with me, but you need more of a life than an old hermit can give you. You'll do fine, just come back to see me. I'll always be here.*

Are you, Grandpa? Are you here? Perrie wondered.

Perrie tilted her head and looked up the rugged

trunk of the old tree, looked up through the branches that time had not conquered.

And for a moment she thought she saw her grandfather's wink in a ray of sunlight arcing down, warming her shoulders.

She drew in a deep breath and bowed her head, pulling Davey close. "Grandpa, I love you."

Davey whispered beside her, "I love you, too, Grandpa Cy."

Perrie bit her lip against another rush of tears. But as she lifted her head, she saw an eagle glide just past the other side of the aged spruce. "Look, Davey. I think Grandpa sent us a messenger." She pointed to the magnificent bird, and together they watched him glide.

"I feel him here, Davey. I think he heard us."

"I'm sorry you're sad."

"It's all right, sweetie. Sometimes love hurts, but there's nothing better in this world than knowing love."

"Let's go tell Mitch we found Grandpa Cy, Mom, okay?" Restless again, Davey darted off toward the trees. "Let's go see if he's back at the cabin yet."

"Davey, we—" But she felt too raw to discuss the temporary nature of Mitch's presence. She sighed, feeling the cold wind beginning to cut through the layers of her clothes. "All right," she conceded. "Let's go make something hot to drink."

He was off like a shot, disappearing into the trees.

"Don't run, Davey. The ground is too slick."

But Davey was already out of sight.

"Davey, come back!" she cried out louder. "Stay with me—"

And then she heard the panicked scream.

Too cold to stay away from the cabin forever, Mitch neared the clearing, frowning at the footprints he could see in the snow, leading away from the cabin. Two sets, and not that fresh—what was Perrie thinking? She and Davey had no business out in this cold, even if the sun was shining.

Though he could understand cabin fever. He never minded being alone, but with the two of them...the cabin's walls seemed to shrink by the day. He'd been gone for hours, simply to avoid being in there with them.

To avoid wishing for what he would never have.

He frowned as he ascended the stairs, kicking the snow off his boots before he entered. He removed them, along with his outerwear, then draped his jacket over a kitchen chair.

A fire still blazed merrily in the hearth. Perrie must have built it up before she left. The scent of something cooking perfumed the air. He glanced toward the stove, seeing the big pot simmering on the back of it.

What would it feel like to come home to this all the time, having Davey run to greet him, Perrie turning to him with a smile?

For a moment he savored the image. Hopes he'd

never let himself contemplate rose to taunt him. Perrie in his arms. In his bed, those delicate hands stroking across his body. Burying himself in her deep…losing themselves in each other.

And raising that boy, teaching him all the things Mitch had learned. Never, ever, turning his back on Davey, no matter what he did.

He slammed one hand against the mantel. *Stop thinking about things that can't happen.*

After all these years, why would he let old, buried longings surface, let them slice deep into a heart that should remain carefully cold, relentlessly neutral?

Love was not his lot in life. He didn't want it. Losing it hurt too much. The only way to be sure was to bury feelings—*all* feelings—so deep they would never surface.

Don't let your anger win, Mitch. He could still hear his mother's voice…still feel the blood too warm on fingers clutching her desperately against him.

Mitch cursed violently against the old pain that could tear his heart from his chest.

I will not care. Never again.

Shaking his head to dislodge thoughts that could only bring harm, Mitch turned away from the fire and glanced around the room, wondering how long they'd been gone.

But only because they were under his roof. Only for Cy's sake.

Not for his.

And then he spied the scrap of paper leaning against the salt and pepper shakers on the scarred wooden table.

"We've gone to Grandpa," it said, in a delicate, very feminine script. "Back soon."

To Grandpa? And then he knew. They were at the grandfather spruce. But those tracks were hours old, and the spruce was only fifteen minutes away, even in this snow.

Something shivered down Mitch's spine, and he fought it. Perrie was a grown woman—but her strength wasn't up to full speed yet. She knew this area—but not in winter. And it was going to be dark in a couple of hours.

He jerked his down jacket back on, muttering beneath his breath. Damn troublesome woman—so like her not to think of anyone but herself.

But even as he thought it, he knew it was a lie. He couldn't explain why she hadn't come when Cy needed her, but he'd seen a gentle soul where he'd expected one hard as brass.

Whatever was going on with Perrie, however little idea he had of what to do with Davey's mother, he had to make sure the boy was safe. He couldn't live with himself if he didn't.

Mitch stalked to the door, donned his boots, gloves and cap, and headed out, grabbing a few supplies and stuffing them in a pack, hoping that he was worrying about nothing.

Perrie pressed against the stitch in her side as she ran through the trees, screaming Davey's name.

"Where are you? Talk to me!" she called out.

There was no answer, and her heart almost burst from her chest.

Oh, please...please don't take him from me. Please don't let him be hurt. Please—not my baby—

Her gaze darted wildly around her. In her panic, she ran this way and that, trying to figure out where the scream had come from.

Though it slammed against every instinct she had, Perrie forced herself to stop and draw a deep breath, trying to stem the panic that overran rational thought.

She closed her eyes for a second, then reopened them. *All right. Stop. Look around you. Think.*

Tracks. *Of course, Perrie. Follow his tracks.* Pulling in another draft of frigid air, she forced herself to calm and slowly scan the landscape. Nothing.

She turned back toward where she'd been, walking several paces, heart sinking to her feet before she saw them.

Small footprints, heading off to the left.

Steeling herself not to give in to fear, Perrie clasped her hands together, her every sense intent upon her son.

"Davey—" she called out. "Where are you?"

Still no answer. *Oh, God—please don't let him be hurt or—*

Mitch. She'd sell her soul to have Mitch here to

help her, but she didn't dare go back to find him. He'd been gone for hours to who knew where.

No, it was up to her. She had to find Davey. And if he— Her mind balked at the thought. He would be all right. He had to be. He just couldn't hear her. She'd find him and those blue eyes would be dancing with mischief. He'd just hidden from her, that was it.

He'd been cooped up too long for an active boy. He would be all right—he was just on an adventure.

She would put him in the corner for disobeying the rules. He was never to wander away in a strange place.

Except that all she wanted was to hold him, to cuddle him close and never, ever let him out of her sight again.

"Davey—" she called out again. "Please, baby, let me know where you are—"

Then finally she heard it, the faint sound of a voice.

A child's voice. Her heart was thumping so hard she couldn't hear.

"Davey, where are you?" She stood very still, every sense alert.

Finally she heard it again. Faint. Strained. But her beloved child's voice.

Perrie took off running toward the sound. Beyond a clump of trees, she skidded to a stop, her breath kicking up in her chest.

The edge of a cliff lay in front of her, a pocket gouged out in the snow.

Like someone had fallen.

"Davey?"

"Mom—" The voice was faint, cracking with strain, but it was him. It was Davey.

She had to hold herself back from rushing to the edge.

"I'm here, sweetheart. Are you hurt?"

"Mom, I fell—" His voice was thready and filled with tears.

"Hold on, sweetie. I'm almost there." With careful steps, she felt her way ahead of her, unsure where the weak spot began.

Finally she neared the edge and lay down in the snow, easing forward.

Oh, no. Oh, please— She couldn't reach him from here.

"Mom?" He lay sprawled on his back, but at the sight of her, he struggled to rise.

"No, Davey, don't—" He lay on a small ledge, about ten feet below her. Only about four feet wide—and past him lay only thin air. "Don't move, sweetie." She could hear her voice shaking as she scanned frantically for a way to get down to him.

But she could see nothing that would work.

"I'm scared." He didn't sound right, she thought.

"Tell me what hurts."

"My chest—it kinda hurts to breathe." Again he struggled to rise. "Come get me, Mom."

She closed her eyes for a second and swallowed against the terror. "I will, just as soon as I can.

You just lie still and don't move." She didn't know if he was aware of how close he was to unthinkable disaster. But she was, and it turned her voice sharp. "No matter what, don't you move an inch, Davey. Not one inch, do you hear me?"

Every cell in her body cried out to be down there with him. She needed a rope, needed—

Help. Needed Mitch. But she had no idea where he was. She'd never tackled anything like this before, but it couldn't wait for Mitch.

"Davey, sweetheart—" Could she do this? Could she leave him to go get the supplies she'd need to save him? All she could see in her mind's eye was him moving, rolling over, losing his balance and tumbling to his death. She couldn't possibly leave him—but he would die in the cold if she didn't. Night would be here soon, and he would not survive a night out in this frigid air.

She felt panic rising, its steel claws climbing up her throat, pushing a helpless despair through her body.

"Davey?" With every ounce of control she possessed, she forced her voice steady. "Sweetheart, I need you to make me a promise. Are you listening?"

"Yes." But his voice sounded so small. So helpless.

She couldn't think about that now. "I have to go back to the cabin to get a rope. You have to lie there very still and not move. Not an inch, do you hear me?"

"Don't leave me, Mom. I'm scared. It's cold."

Perrie clasped her hands on her head so tightly it felt like it might crack. The war within her threatened to split her apart.

He will die if you don't get him up from there.

But he might roll over and—

A thousand 'mights' raced through her head. Every maternal instinct she possessed kept her immobilized against leaving him alone for a second.

Her stomach heaved with terror. But she had to stay calm. Had to convince him. Had to force herself to leave.

"Sweetie, I know you're scared. And cold. But I have to get you up from there. I can't reach you where you are. It won't take me very long to get to the cabin and back, and then I'll get you up." How, she didn't know yet, but she'd do it. No matter how hard it was.

"Get Mitch. Mitch can save me."

Oh, honey, if only you knew how badly I wish he were here. "Maybe Mitch will be back when I get there, but even if he's not, I'll get you up. Don't worry, all right? Just be very, very still, Davey. Do you hear me? You can't move from where you are."

"I wish you could stay here and tell me a story until Mitch comes."

"Mitch doesn't know where we are right now, but I'll leave him a note, okay? And I'll be back in just a very few minutes."

"Mom?" His voice reached out to hold her, fear

threaded with need. "Can you tell me a little bit of a story first?"

Perrie pressed her hand over her lips to keep from crying out. Swallowing hard, she grasped for control. "Okay—just a little bit. Then I really have to go, sweetie."

"Okay." His voice seemed fainter.

For a second, Perrie wanted to scream. How could she possibly think of a story at a time like this? But she had to. It might be the last story she ever told—

No. It would not be. She would make her point to Davey with this story, and then she would race to the cabin and back.

"Okay." She sucked in a draft of frigid air. "Remember Ermengilda and her friend Henry?"

"Yeah—"

"Well, one day they and another fish named Gloria were swimming around too close to a boat. She and Gloria got caught and pulled from the water, but Henry swam away. Ermengilda felt like she couldn't breathe and she knew they had to get back in the water soon or they would die. She couldn't panic. Instead, she had to think. Gloria wasn't doing so well, though. She was screaming and thrashing around where they'd been set down, not too far from the water.

"Ermengilda knew that their goose was cooked if they didn't figure out a solution—quick. 'Gloria, be quiet,' she whispered. 'Be still. Play dead. Then when they're not looking, we'll get away.'

"But Gloria wouldn't listen. She kept thrashing around so much that Ermengilda was afraid she'd draw their attention. The next thing Ermengilda knew, Gloria was being yanked up and put in some kind of bucket. But while they were looking away, Ermengilda managed to get back in the water where Henry was waiting, and they swam away, back to their mothers."

"So what happened to Gloria?"

"They never knew. She didn't come back. If she hadn't panicked, if she'd just been very still like Ermengilda told her to do, she could have gone back home and been all right."

"That's what you want me to do, Mom? Be very still?"

Perrie pressed one fist to her chest, against an aching heart. "Yes, sweetie. It's very important. I know you're cold and I know you're scared, but I need you to be brave like you were when you went to find help for me. Only, this time, I'm the one who has to find the tools I need so I can get you up and then take you back to the cabin."

"And Mitch. Bring Mitch back."

"If he's anywhere around, I'll find him. But I'll get you up, with or without Mitch, do you understand? It won't be long, so just be very, very still." He looked so small, so helpless. She forced a smile to her face. "Everything will be fine, I promise."

His blue eyes had never looked bigger. He had never looked more precious...or more fragile.

"Okay. I'll be very still."

She blew him a kiss. "Hold that kiss for me, okay? I want one back when I get you up here."

"Okay."

"I love you, sweetheart." She could feel a sob rising up from within her. With all her strength, she pushed it back down. "It will be just fine. I'll get you up and then we'll go make some hot chocolate. You can have as many marshmallows as you want, all right?"

"Okay. I love you, too, Mom."

"I'll be back very soon. And don't worry if you hear me calling out for Mitch. I'll get you up, but if I can find him, we can do it sooner."

"Bring Mitch. He can do anything, Mom."

Tears blurring her vision so much she could hardly see him, Perrie nodded. "I'll be back, sweetie. You're doing great."

It took every ounce of strength she had to push herself away from the edge, to leave behind the child who was her heart.

It felt like someone had tied a lead anchor to her chest and every step away from where Davey lay ripped her insides open a little more.

But she had no choice. Once she forced herself to turn away, Perrie began to run. When she'd gotten a number of yards away, she began to call out for Mitch, trying to keep the terror from her voice in case Davey could hear her.

Chapter Nine

They'd definitely been here, the tracks mingling like a herd of animals had stampeded. Perrie's tracks weren't so numerous, but Davey's were all over the place. Mitch squinted, trying to make out a pattern, a sense of urgency pushing at him.

He was concentrating so hard he almost missed the sound.

His name?

Mitch froze, listening.

There it was again. Perrie's voice calling out. Even at this distance, something about it dug claws into his belly.

He leapt into action, answering her. "I'm here. Perrie. Stand still and call out again."

"Mitch?" No question. Terror shaded her voice, turning it from gentle to sharp.

Then he saw her. Alone. He turned in her direction.

"Mitch—oh thank God—" She ran straight toward him, her motion jerky with fear. "It's Davey—he's fallen. Oh please, Mitch, help me. Help him. He's—"

He reached her and pulled her into his arms. She was chalk-white, her eyes almost black with fear. "What's happened?" He could feel her small frame shudder as her teeth chattered. Pulling her closer to warm her, he pressed her into his chest.

For a moment she clung to him, then jerked away, looking up at him with horror in her eyes. "He's fallen off the edge. He's on a little ledge, and I can't reach him. He's—oh God, I have to get back—" She turned to run, pulling away from him.

Mitch didn't try to stop her. Instead he took off running in the direction she was headed, grasping her arm and pulling her along with him. "Is he hurt?"

She shook her head. "I can't tell. He says his chest hurts."

"Maybe he just got the wind knocked out of him. Anything turned oddly, his legs or arms?"

She was sobbing for breath now. "Not that I could tell. Oh, Mitch, he's so scared. I didn't want to leave him, but I had to—"

"Of course you did. It's going to be dark soon, and he can't spend the night on that ledge."

She shot him a grateful look, but she couldn't spare much breath. He wanted to tell her to stop, to conserve her strength, but Davey had to be the prime concern right now. He'd just have to watch her closely.

Then they were there, and he could see the spot where Davey had slid over the side.

"Davey, I found Mitch," Perrie called out, dropping to her knees and starting to scramble toward the edge.

Mitch grabbed her arm, shaking his head. Speaking low, he cautioned her. "Stay back. Let me look. We don't know how much weight it can handle or where it's weak." In a louder voice, he called out, keeping his voice deliberately light. "Hey, buddy, decided to see if you could be Jim Bridger and explore the cliffs?"

"Mitch!" The little voice wobbled, then strengthened. "I told Mom you would save me."

Mitch had never been so glad to hear a voice in his life.

"You bet I will," Mitch answered, scanning the area. "Just hold on right where you are, and we'll have you up in no time." To Perrie he nodded toward the edge and spoke more quietly. "Stay back here, but talk to him while I get ready."

Her eyes were still huge with fear, but she nodded gamely. "How are you doing, sweetie?"

"I'm being real still, like Ermie was."

A ghost of a smile crossed Perrie's lips, her eyes

bright with tears. "That's Princess Ermie to you, pal."

When Davey gave a faint, broken giggle, Mitch's heart gave a twist. Ruthlessly he tuned them out. No time for emotion now.

He found the tree he wanted and tied a bowline knot to hold the rope he'd taken from his pack. With fierce concentration, he formed a series of knots for handholds. He inched toward the edge on his belly. When he neared the edge, snow and a few rocks tumbled over. "How you doing, sport?"

"I'm okay." The little voice wasn't steady, but Mitch heard no panic.

What a guy. A man would be lucky to have a son like this one. Mitch leaned over the edge—and damn near choked at the sight.

But he revealed none of his concern. "Hey, fella." There was barely enough room for Davey, much less for someone his own size. But at least he'd brought enough rope.

Davey stirred, trying to sit up.

"Don't move yet." He forced his voice to remain steady while he scanned the cliff face between him and Davey. "Just lie back and play possum."

Davey's face lit. "Like you told me how they play dead so their enemies don't bother them?"

"That's right. Pretend I'm a big grizzly and I need a snack for supper. A boy like you would be just about a good snack."

Davey giggled, the sound a little stronger.

"I've still got my bear, Mitch. He's in my pocket."

"Good for you." Mitch met Perrie's gaze, the air between them thick with fear, but her eyes signaled gratitude. He smiled to reassure her and saw her visibly relax.

She didn't need to know how dicey this would be.

"Davey, are you sick at your stomach?"

"No, but my bottom hurts where I landed."

"Can you move your arms and legs?"

"Yes, sir."

"All right. I want you to try something, but stop if anything hurts. Try it very slowly, just a little bit at first. Can you move your arms and legs like you were making a snow angel?" He heard Perrie's breath catch behind him. His own breath stilled as he waited. "Slow now—don't make any sudden movements. Just try your arms first."

He stared as Davey moved gingerly. When Davey spread his arms out and didn't meet thin air, he seemed to draw strength, his eyes brightening.

"That's good." Mitch heard Perrie's soft inhalation behind him. "Now try your legs the same way. Slowly at first."

Davey's legs straightened, then began to move. "Can I get up now?"

"No!" His voice was too sharp, but he'd seen Davey's enthusiasm carry him away before. "Now slowly again, just move your head a tiny bit from side to side." Davey complied. "Does that hurt any?"

The boy shook his head.

"That's good. Try it a little bit more. Look over at the side of the cliff."

Davey's head turned fluidly.

"Still doesn't hurt?"

"No, sir."

Mitch wanted to shout in thanksgiving. "Now try the other side. Still okay?"

"Uh-huh. I mean, yes, sir."

Mitch's throat tightened. "Okay. Hold on a minute. Don't move." For one second, he broke eye contact to turn his head and nod at Perrie.

She was still bone-white, one hand covering her mouth. But she nodded back, her frame easing slightly.

He turned back to Davey. "All right. Now listen to me carefully and don't move until I tell you."

"I won't." Trust rang in Davey's voice.

Mitch clamped down hard on the emotions that threatened to burst free. Emotions were his enemy, and right now they were Davey's enemy, too. A lifetime's worth of maneuvering out of tight spots was about to pay off.

"I want you to stay on your back and scoot over toward the cliff wall very slowly. Can you do that? Don't roll over. Just scoot on your back as close as you can to the rocks."

Davey began to inch away from the dangerous edge, clearing a space that, with luck, would allow enough room for Mitch to land. Mitch felt like he could breathe a little easier with every inch that appeared between the boy and thin air.

"Very good, son. Now, if it still doesn't hurt, I want you to roll over and face the cliff, then cover your head with your arms. I'm going to come down, and some pieces of rock may break loose. I need you to protect your head, and don't look up, no matter what happens."

"Davey, pull your hood up over your head, too."

Perrie kept her voice very calm, but when Mitch turned to ready himself to descend, he could see the strain in her face. Everything in her cried out to do something, he could tell. There was nothing worse than being helpless to save someone you loved.

Mitch understood that feeling only too well.

He kept his voice low so only she could hear. "I'm bringing him back up safely. You can take that to the bank." He was *not* losing one more person he cared about.

Face tight with strain, she nodded. "I believe you."

Deep within Mitch, gratitude warred with his past. She didn't know how badly he'd failed before. But he would not let her faith be misplaced.

With a quick nod, he descended as carefully as he'd ever done anything in his life, silently willing the rock face to hold and cursing every pebble that didn't. "I'm on my way, Davey. You just hold on a little bit longer."

A tiny muffled voice answered, "Okay, Mitch."

Then finally he was down, with barely enough room to kneel beside the boy. He peeled Davey away from the rock face and drew him into his arms.

"I got him, Perrie."

Davey latched on to him as if he'd been gone for years.

Mitch sat down against the rock face and cradled the boy tightly, giving thanks for a grace he didn't deserve.

When he thought he could speak without his voice breaking, he nudged Davey's chin upward. "You'd better tell your mom you're okay."

"I'm safe, Mom. Mitch has me now."

Mitch bit the inside of his cheek and looked away.

"Let me check you out," he said hoarsely. But when he tried to peel the boy away enough, Davey clung to him like a tick. "It's okay," he soothed. "I won't let you fall. I just need to be sure everything's okay." With a quick scan, he checked Davey's pupils and felt his limbs, then called out loudly. "He's going to have some really nice bruises, Perrie, but I don't think anything is seriously hurt."

"Thank God." Her voice came from above them, quivering slightly.

"Okay, sport. Now we have to climb back up. You ready for a little adventure?"

Davey's eyes were as big as saucers, his small arms tight around Mitch as he clung. Something slow and sweet moved inside Mitch's chest. But faith shone in Davey's gaze as he nodded, his voice only quavering slightly. "Yes, sir."

"I'm going to put you on my back the way you like to ride, but I'm going to rope you against me so you can't slip."

Davey nodded.

Mitch had to smile, speaking gently. "First, son, you're going to have to let go."

Davey nodded again but didn't move. Then he squared his little shoulders and moved away, if only a few inches.

"That's right. Edge around to my back." Mitch scooted away from the rock face. "Want to practice tying the knots I taught you?"

The voice grew smaller. "I'd rather let you."

Mitch chuckled. "That's just fine. You can practice more when we get back."

"Mitch?" A small head brushed his neck.

"What?"

"I'm sorry. I didn't mean to fall."

Mitch swallowed. "I know you didn't."

"Mom didn't get mad. You're not mad?"

Mitch turned, the ropes not yet tight around them. He looked straight into the uncertain blue gaze. "I'm not mad." But his voice warned, "I don't want you ever running off alone again, though. These mountains are not a playground."

The blond head ducked. "Yes, sir. I promise I won't."

Mitch nudged Davey's chin upward. "I know

you won't.'' Mitch smiled, and a small smile greeted his.

His chest tightened, but Mitch steeled himself against feeling too much. ''All right. Let's get this show on the road.''

Fingers that had been cold for too many hours rebelled, but Mitch simply ignored them and forced his body to respond as he needed, refusing to acknowledge the cold or the fact that he hadn't eaten since this morning. This was all that mattered, the little body that nestled against him, this little boy believing that Mitch would get them back up safely.

And he would. This time would be different. He wouldn't let his emotions win—he would win this time, by keeping himself carefully neutral, concentrating only on the next step, pulling them up to the next knot on the rope.

Finally they could see Perrie. Worry and fear gave way to joy on her lovely face. Mitch could see her straining against the urge to run to her son, but she held fast and stayed back as he'd asked.

At last they were over the top and safely away from the edge. Perrie dropped to her knees beside them, reaching for Davey, throwing her arms around both of them.

Mitch could feel her trembling. His own hands were none too steady as he untied the knots binding Davey to him. Once Davey was free, he scrambled into his mother's arms, finally giving in to his tears. Mitch felt the loss of her touch as she gathered Davey close.

Perrie rocked him, her eyes squeezed tightly shut. Then she opened them and looked at Mitch, her gaze naked and vulnerable as she gripped Davey so tightly her knuckles were white.

A lifetime passed in seconds as Mitch felt himself opening to her, too. It was as though they stood there together, at the edge of something that touched at the heart of existence.

Mitch ached with a power far beyond what had strained his muscles, had stretched his control, had unraveled the edges of his distance.

For a moment he felt the pull of belonging. Felt that something powerful and private had happened to them, which would leave them never again the same.

Then he snapped back to reality, to who he really was—and what was possible for a man like him.

For all that he knew Perrie's terror, shared the sense of narrow escape from an unbearable loss, Mitch also knew that the sharing was only temporary.

He was, as he had been, on the outside looking in. No matter how precious the child had felt, clinging to him, no matter how his heart had reached out when Perrie had drawn them both close—he was temporary. A port of call on a journey that would carry them away. Perrie and Davey would always share the bond that, for a few brief moments, he had been privileged to touch.

They would forever be together. And he would forever be alone.

If the thought ripped into his too-open heart, Mitch still accepted what must be. He rose quickly and gathered his gear, itching to get away, to be by himself.

"We'd better get back." Too curt, but he couldn't afford softness now.

Perrie flinched from his tone. Rising to her knees, she held on to Davey, who had settled into exhaustion against her.

"Here, let me carry him," Mitch offered, reaching out.

She pulled back and shook her head, climbing shakily to her feet.

He put out a hand and steadied her, then stood carefully back. "If you get tired, let me know." He picked up his gear and started off.

Perrie's legs felt like cooked spaghetti, but she clung tightly to Davey and concentrated on the ground in front of her.

When she tripped again, Mitch plucked Davey from her arms. "Don't be foolish. You don't have anything to prove. You're out on your feet."

She wanted to protest, but it was all she could do to keep walking. In the adrenaline's wake, she was a rag doll whose stuffing had vanished.

"Come here." Mitch pulled her into his side. She resisted only because he was already loaded down with Davey and his gear. She should be able to walk back by herself, but she wanted nothing more than to crawl into his arms right beside her son.

Thinking about what could have happened still had the power to unnerve her completely. If Mitch hadn't come after them…if he hadn't been there at all…

Perrie shuddered and grabbed on to Mitch's waist, squeezing her eyes shut. When his arm tightened around her shoulder, she wanted to weep in relief.

But she couldn't. She had to keep a lid on her own emotions so that Davey wouldn't be traumatized by her terror. Had to calmly check her son over, once she could remove his clothes. Had to feed him and get him into bed.

But all she could see when she closed her eyes was that ledge and the horrible drop just inches away from him.

Her fingers squeezed convulsively into Mitch's side.

"It's okay," he soothed. "It's over."

But it wasn't. This experience had just brought home how impossible it would be for her to stay here with Davey, even if Mitch were willing to give over the cabin. She'd been a fool to even consider it. She might be able to take care of herself up here through a long winter, but there were too many dangers waiting to snap Davey up in their ravening maws.

She would have to leave, no question now. And soon, before winter trapped them. The thought made her tired.

And sad. Because they would have to leave

Mitch behind. No matter how much she knew it would be better for him not to get embroiled in her nightmare with Simon, she couldn't help feeling the loss already.

Davey would miss him, but he would not be the only one.

"Okay, here we are," Mitch said.

The cabin was only a few feet away, and a sense of homecoming swept over Perrie. She'd never seen a sight more welcome in her life—except for the sight of Mitch when Davey had been in danger.

She forced herself to straighten and make the steps alone, opening the door for Mitch and his burdens. Once inside, Mitch laid Davey on the sofa, and she busied herself undressing him. Exhausted from his ordeal, Davey barely stirred.

Mitch hovered close, checking his toes and fingers for signs of frostbite. "I think we got him in time."

She glanced back over her shoulder at him. Dark eyes gone soft as velvet studied her son, then turned to look at her.

She couldn't breathe. He surrounded her like a fortress, his strength her bulwark, his broad shoulders so close and tempting. She gazed at his mouth, so close to hers, then looked up into eyes turned to smoldering coals.

The moment spun out, trembling with something momentous. Around them, the air crackled with electrifying promise.

Mitch tore his gaze away, releasing her from the spell that had held her motionless.

She turned back to her child, pulling off his shirt, crying out softly. "Oh, Davey," she whispered, but her child slept on.

Mitch had been right. Davey would sport quite a sampling of bruises, but the layers of clothing she'd forced him to wear had protected him so that no skin was broken.

"I checked his pupils when we were down on the ledge. They were even and responded to the light. I couldn't find any broken skin on his head," Mitch said.

"I don't feel any puffy places. I should probably make him wake up to be sure."

"Yeah. Let's see if he'll eat some of that stew that smells so good. Then we can put him to bed. Kids are pretty resilient. Boone and I got caught jumping off the barn once, even farther than Davey fell. I decided I could fly and missed the hay I was aiming to hit. I saw stars for a while, but they never even had to take me to the doctor. But if you want, we can leave now and head to Pinedale. It'll take us several hours, but we can get him looked at."

Perrie gnawed at her lip. "I don't really want to get him out in the cold again, but—"

Then Davey stirred. "Mom? Mitch?" He sat up and looked around. "Wow, that really happened, didn't it? You climbed down about a hundred feet and saved me!"

Mitch chuckled softly. "Not so far as all that."

"I tried to grab on to that branch, but I slipped."

"Did you hit your head when you fell?"

Davey shook his head. "No. I landed on my bottom. But then I felt kinda dizzy when I looked out over the edge, so I laid down real quick."

"How do you feel now?" Perrie asked.

"Kinda achy, like when I fell off the swing set last year, remember?"

Perrie smiled, relief seeping in. She turned to Mitch. "Davey has always had a real affinity for falling on his very hard head. So far, nothing seems to have scrambled his brains." She thought for a minute. "Let's just keep an eye on him tonight."

Mitch nodded, his face impassive again.

"Mom, I'm hungry," Davey wheedled.

She pulled his shirt back over his head, feeling the laughter bubble up inside her. "So what's new?" She straightened it around his middle and gripped his shoulders.

"You will never scare me like that again, right?"

Davey cut his glance over to Mitch. "Mitch already told me not to wander away. He said I should apologize, too." Davey looked truly penitent. "I'm really sorry, Mom."

She swallowed the lump that rose in her throat every time she thought of what a close call it had been. "We owe Mitch a very big thank-you."

Davey smiled and launched himself off the sofa into Mitch's arms. "Mitch is the greatest, Mom. Didn't I tell you?"

The sight of the big man cradling her son so

close made Perrie ache for all that her son deserved
and had never had, chief among them the love of a
good man like this one.

She ached for the same thing. But she knew it
wouldn't happen. Mitch had made it amply clear
that he lived alone. Free to drift.

She pushed to her feet to get away from the longing swelling up, threatening to burst free. "I'll dish
up some stew for all of us."

On shaky legs she moved across the room.

Chapter Ten

Perrie came out of the room she and Davey shared, looking wan and exhausted. She hesitated in the doorway, as though disturbed by Mitch's presence.

"I can go in my room if you'd rather be alone," he offered.

She shook her head quickly. "That's not necessary." But her steps were slow as she crossed the room, settling herself on the rug in front of the fire. Her movements were careful. Brittle as though she hovered close to breaking.

Mitch tried to give her the space she obviously needed, but his book couldn't hold his attention. When he read the same sentence four times in a row, he finally looked up, about to ask if she wanted to play cards or something.

Even from the back, he could tell that she was holding herself together by a thread. Arms wrapped around her waist, her back curled like a protective shell, she shook with silent sobs.

He should let her be, should stay away from temptation.

But he could not.

Mitch abandoned his book, moving to her side and pulling her onto his lap, wrapping his arms around her.

"I just keep thinking about what would have happened if you hadn't been here—" She stared into the fire, tears streaming from her eyes. One small, delicate hand dashed at the tears in vain, a persistent scrubbing that could not stem the tide.

She was so valiant. So small, yet so strong. It hurt him to see her so devastated.

"You would have figured something out."

Perrie shook her head. "He could have died, and it would have been my fault." A deep shudder wracked her fragile frame, and Mitch tightened his arms around her.

For a moment she tried to hold herself apart. Then with a broken sob, she surrendered. She leaned into his chest, sliding her arms around him, her hands gripping the back of his shirt as tightly as Davey had held him when he'd reached the ledge.

It felt like heaven. Like home. Like everything he'd ever wanted. And everything he would never have.

"Perrie," he groaned.

She lifted her head from his shoulder, her face only a breath from his own.

Within her, he saw an answering need. A need for refuge, for sanctuary from the cold darkness. A loneliness that just might match his own.

The last vestiges of his conscious mind knew that this was a bad idea. He fought to remember why.

But his damnable heart didn't care. He'd been so long alone. So long adrift from human connection. For just one moment, he wanted to warm himself at her sweet fire.

Just one moment—was it so much to ask?

Her lake-blue eyes beckoned him closer, pulling him in. And finally he could stay in the darkness no longer. He lowered his mouth to hers, aching to feed on the sweetness every cell in his body craved.

Sweetness was there, yes. A shy, soft pressure. Tentative. Almost virginal.

But how could that be? She'd been married, borne a child. Yet something about her was almost—

Frightened.

She drew back, a scant breath away. He felt her tremble, like a doe poised for flight.

Was she afraid of him?

Of course she was. His heart clenched. She could tell, somehow. Knew that he was all wrong for love.

I won't hurt you, he wanted to say. But he had broken that promise before. He tensed, readying himself to set her away.

And then a miracle happened. Perrie drew in a deep breath and leaned into him, sealing his mouth with hers. The innocent trust in her lips brought a tightness to his chest. He battled the need fighting to crush her close. To ravish. To possess. The endless darkness inside him cried out for haste.

Instead, he beat it back. Carefully he increased the pressure of his mouth, wooing her like he would a wounded creature in need of his care.

Perrie's lips opened slightly, her breath warm against his. Mitch slid one hand upward to cradle her head, almost afraid to breathe lest he frighten her away.

Then she arched against him, tasting him with one tentative sweep of her tongue.

Soul-deep craving rocked him. Mitch felt a shiver begin deep inside him, from a place where he'd long ago buried hope.

With a white-knuckled grip on his hunger, Mitch held on tight, feeling as green and new as an untried boy. When Perrie relaxed against him, her fingers stroking his neck, her breasts pressing against his chest, Mitch felt something inside him unfurl. Desire, yes—so hot and dark, it was all he could do not to let the beast loose.

But there was more. Her artless caresses stirred a tenderness he'd never known. He glimpsed a new world where he was a virgin himself.

Craving rocked him to the core. Sharp claws of need tore his flesh open, throat to belly. He'd been a long time without a woman's sweet dark heat, and he could barely hold back.

But he would, somehow. This was not about his need. This was about hers. Perrie deserved a gentle hand. He would do this right or die trying.

Holding tight to the chains of his craving, Mitch lifted an unsteady hand to stroke her face while he deepened the kiss. A featherlight touch over the pale shell of her ear. A slow stroke down the delicate line of her throat.

Perrie's head drifted back as she welcomed his touch, every stroke sending flares through her body. Never had she been touched like this, like something precious, something worthy of care. She wanted to watch Mitch as he stroked her, wanted to see what was on his face.

But it felt so exquisite, and she was so hungry. She could not take the chance that he might stop.

So she leaned back into his strong arms and welcomed his caress. Something new awoke deep inside the woman who had only known sex as a power struggle she always lost. A molasses-thick warmth spread within her, tendrils unfurling from low in her belly. She arched her back against his arm, wanting to open herself up to this man, to take a chance. To see where he would lead her.

So she did, letting her head fall back, her breasts rising, silently begging for his touch.

She felt the tension in him, the coiled strength, the potent male power held tightly in check. But for how long? For a moment her breath hitched. She knew what it was to be powerless, to be used by someone stronger. And Mitch was far stronger than the man who had taught her that sex was a weapon.

Like the lash of a whip, Perrie jerked up, doubled over, her back to Mitch, her fear a venom poisoning the air around them.

The big hands dropped away, setting her aside, instantly free.

And Perrie was ashamed. This was Mitch, not Simon. This was the man who had saved her child's life, who had nursed her to health.

Slowly she turned her head, seeing naked devastation on the once-harsh face staring into the fire. His powerful body tensed to rise and walk away.

She couldn't let that happen. Not to him. Not to herself. They stood at the precipice of something....

She put her hand on one arm, rigid with muscle.

His gaze glanced across her, closing down as she watched.

What to say? How to explain? Perrie swallowed deeply, knowing the treachery of words.

So, instead, she took action, sliding her hand up his arm to caress his hard jaw. Tense...rigid...he only cut her a wary glance.

And her woman's heart realized that he was as afraid of her as she was of him.

It was a novel thought, so incredible as to be almost beyond conceiving. But as she pondered, something told her she was right. Mitch might be physically far stronger, but hadn't she seen often enough that the hard shell covered a heart capable of great tenderness? Hadn't he shown her a hundred times just how different he was from Simon?

She knew he'd been alone most of his life. Had seen his longing, the traces of a hunger he would not admit.

A hunger he'd continue to deny if she gave up here and let cowardice win. Thinking of all the ways in which he'd shown that the hard loner was only a façade, Perrie drew on the strength that had gotten her this far—

And took a chance.

She met his gaze and refused to release it. With unsteady fingers, she reached for the top button of her peach velour shirt, working it open.

Mitch's hot gaze followed her hands. As she bared her body, she saw his nostrils flare, his hands clench tight. His gaze shot up to study hers. She forced herself not to look away, then slowly leaned toward him, bringing her mouth within a breath of his.

Just before their lips touched, he spoke her name, his voice as much question as moan.

She had no words, so she answered with her lips, pressing a kiss to his mouth, opening to him and touching her tongue to his lips.

Fire shot through Mitch's body, fire and a spark of hope. He pulled her down again, spreading her across his lap, his fingers driving into her hair as his tongue slid into the dark sweetness of her mouth.

Thrown from a foretaste of heaven to the empty

void and back, Mitch reeled off balance like a top skidding across a rocky floor. He grasped for the control that had saved his life, but it was lost in the bright flare of Perrie's kiss, the fine promise of her flesh pressing against his.

The image of her pale hands working at the fabric, baring the tender valley between her breasts—

Mitch groaned and took the kiss deeper.

And she responded like no woman he'd ever known. Fire tinged with innocence, heat layered with honey. She arched against him again, a soft moan against his kiss, her fingers sliding into his hair and pulling him closer still.

Mitch forgot all the reasons why this could not happen. Forgot why he should walk away. In the honeyed darkness of Perrie's kiss, he found a dream. Tomorrow would still be tomorrow, but tonight he needed only her, only this.

Sliding his hand up her body, he worked at her buttons, baring her to the silken top beneath her shirt. Hard nipples against the soft fabric begged for his touch.

Mitch tore his mouth away from hers and lifted his head, his gaze greedily devouring the sight. He heard her inhale and shifted his eyes to hers, seeing a fragile worry lining her brow.

"You're so beautiful," he soothed, sliding his hand over the silk, coming to rest over the lush contour of her breast, his fingers curving to capture the feel.

She gasped faintly, leaning into his touch, and

Mitch's fingers tightened while edgy, dark need shot down his spine.

He closed his eyes, swallowed hard. He wanted her so badly, wanted her fast and hard and hot. But he had to do this right.

Then, slowly…softly, he circled one finger, tracing her curves, nearing the hard peak of her nipple while he watched her blue eyes darken to navy smoke.

Perrie moaned, and her head fell back over his arm, pressing her breast closer as if begging for his hand. Instead, Mitch brought her his mouth.

When the wet heat closed over her breast, Perrie's moan slid deep into her throat. Her hips bucked, and an unknown hunger wiped thought from her mind. She clutched at his hair, knowing a pleasure from his suckling unlike anything before in her life.

A fever gripped her, an urgency Perrie had never before felt. Her hips rocked upward, and Perrie wanted to scream, wanted to beg, though she didn't know for what.

But Mitch did.

He captured her mouth again, sliding one hand up beneath her silken undershirt, his fingers gliding across skin that put the fabric to shame. Then he tore his mouth from hers while he bared her torso to his gaze.

Perrie felt just the opposite of anything she'd expected to feel. So hot, Mitch's eyes didn't make her want to hide but instead to preen, to display, to invite not only his touch but his gaze. For a woman who had only known shame and degradation before, the feelings Mitch invoked sent power surging through her blood. For the first time in her life, Perrie felt the strength of her womanhood, the electric arc between woman and man.

That arc fed a hunger she'd never felt in her life, and suddenly Perrie wanted to know it all, everything this man could teach her. With fingers made reckless by desire, she gripped his body and pulled him close.

The change in Perrie electrified Mitch, sent his blood singing. The bonds on his own hunger strained, the threads snapping, one by one.

He had to get closer. Had to be inside her. It took everything he had to keep from ripping the clothes from her body.

Perrie's mouth became a weapon, nipping at his lips, suckling at his throat. With a low growl, she scraped her teeth down his neck, her craving pushing his beyond control.

Mitch's fingers unsnapped her jeans, stripping them away until her body was only covered with one small triangle of white cotton.

It was the cotton that stopped him, reminded him that she was fragile, never mind the heat that gripped her now.

Pulling her up to sitting, Mitch grasped her shoulders with his hands, shaking her faintly as she plucked blindly at the buttons on his shirt.

"Perrie," he gritted out. "Stop. I want you too much. I don't want to hurt you."

Blue eyes as deep as the sea met his, shades of trust mingling with fire. "You won't," she declared, and he almost lost it again.

"You don't know that." He had to know that she was aware, not just lost in a sensual fog.

Blue eyes could crackle, he discovered. Biting back a chuckle, he heard her mutter as she worked at his buttons, pulling the tail of his shirt from the waistband of his jeans.

Then she sucked in a breath and ran her nails over his chest, driving all the air from his lungs. He strained for release from the imprisonment of denim.

Mitch clapped his hands over hers as they teased at the hair on his chest. "Wait," he croaked. "I want to see your hair."

She didn't remove her hands but kept them gliding and swirling, burning him with her every touch. But she tossed her head and brought the golden braid sliding over one breast.

His body leapt and his hips rocked toward her, the longing to bury himself almost overcoming his need to see the golden curtain from his dreams.

It took too many tries to remove the band, too many distractions from her rose-tipped breasts rising against the back of his hand. But finally her golden mane flowed loose, as he had dreamed it.

With fingers shaking from desire, he combed through the raw honey silk, spreading the strands over her shoulders, cascading down her torso, hiding the beauty of her breasts behind a gossamer veil.

Firelight limned her frame as he slid off her panties, settling her straddled over his lap. Mitch lifted handfuls of hair, watching them drift across her skin, teasing her breasts with the strands.

Her mound pressed against his hardness, only his jeans keeping them apart. While his body burned, his mind etched the image to hold close, long after she was gone.

He'd never seen anything more beautiful in his life.

Perrie was glad for every minute she'd let her hair grow. Suddenly it wasn't a routine part of her, something to be tucked away and tamed. The look in Mitch's eyes made her feel special…beautiful, like she'd never felt before.

She let her head drop back, felt Mitch tease her skin with her hair. Arching over his legs, she offered her body to him in a way wholly unique in her life. She gloried in her nakedness, felt free and wild.

Leaning back on her hands, she lifted her hips and brushed them over the hard ridge straining at his jeans. He was so big…all over. She should be afraid, but somehow she wasn't.

Through the curtain of her hair, she felt Mitch's mouth close over one breast. One hand slid behind her back to bring her closer; the other slid slowly down her hip and over her belly.

Tantalizing slow touches feathered over her skin, glancing across the tops of her thighs.

His fingers drifted over the heart of her. He pressed against her with his thumb—

And Perrie gasped, sparks shooting over every nerve in her body. She jerked away, then hurriedly pressed back again. His touch felt like heaven.

Slowly he teased her, darting touches away and back, making slow circles that turned her whole body rigid and shaking. Deep inside, Perrie felt something grow, spreading through her body and sharpening a craving unlike anything she'd ever known.

"Mitch?" She wanted to pull away, but she'd die if she did. Then his strong arms laid her back against his legs. He lifted her hips up, his shoulders spreading her wider—

So open. Too open, too vulnerable, too—

His mouth closed over her, and Perrie bucked like she'd been touched with a live wire.

Heat. Aching sweetness. Glory and rapture and sizzling nerves—

So close to something unspeakably beautiful, so nearly painful, Perrie started to panic, too far outside herself, too far out in the open, too alone, too—

His tongue slid inside her, and Perrie flew past the edge of any world she'd ever known.

Mitch's arms held her tightly, his body strong beneath her, his grip never wavering. She was safe, utterly safe—spinning out into the heavens.

When Perrie let go, Mitch felt like he'd won the

biggest victory of his life. As her body shuddered in his arms, he wanted to shout, he felt like he'd been granted the finest reward he would ever know.

Then she fell limp in his arms, and Mitch drew her close, his own hunger less important than sharing this moment when her trust had been his, her faith complete. He gathered her up against him, sliding his hands into the spill of bright hair as she lay boneless across his lap, sighing softly.

He'd done one thing right in his life. For whatever reason, this woman had never felt what she felt right now, he could sense it with every fiber in him. Nothing had ever made him feel so good, so strong. It was almost enough to make him forget the ache that still gripped him.

Perrie slid back from the magical place where Mitch had sent her spiraling, every nerve in her body alive and glowing. But as she returned, she felt the tension in his body and reminded herself that only she had found satisfaction.

She discovered something else new on this startling night. Instead of dreading the need for the man with her to be satisfied, she felt eager. Hungry, even.

Perrie turned in Mitch's arms, fastening her mouth to his throat. When she felt the hum of his groan, she licked her way up his neck, looping one arm around him and bringing him closer.

Against her hip, she felt the pulse of his need. Rising to her knees before him, she clasped his face in her hands and lowered her mouth for a deep, hungry kiss. And though she'd thought herself satiated, she realized that she knew less than nothing. Need, sharp and raw, shot through her body. She wanted him naked, too, wanted to touch him all over. With fingers edgy from need, Perrie tore at the buttons of his jeans.

When the change swept over her features and Perrie's hunger enveloped them both, Mitch felt the renewed bite of his own, the snapping jaws of a need so huge it threatened to consume him. Gritting his teeth to maintain his control, he replaced her fingers with his. In seconds, he had his clothes off, had her spread naked beneath him.

Perrie inhaled sharply, and Mitch jerked his gaze to hers, expecting fear. She was so small, so fragile.

But that's not what he saw. He saw a need that flared as hot as his own.

Mitch covered her body with his, holding his weight with his arms, and took her mouth as he wanted to take her body, fast and hard. Every muscle strained with the screaming power of his craving. He beat it back, but just barely.

"Perrie," he gasped. "I don't know how long I can hold off."

Her smile was his answer as she opened her arms wide. "Don't wait. Please don't wait."

He nudged her legs open, straining to bury himself inside. But he looked at her again, so small against him.

With one smooth motion, he reversed their positions, spreading her across his groin, holding her hips in his hands, brushing the tip of himself against her lush, wet heat. His whole body jolted. "Take me inside you, Perrie," he groaned. "Before I die."

He saw her eyes light, felt her hands grip his shoulders, her knees settle outside his hips.

And then he felt paradise. Wet and warm, so tight he gritted against a pleasure so sharp he thought he would surely perish.

Slowly she slid down his length, and Mitch died a little more with each inch. She rocked her hips and seated him to the hilt.

And then Perrie, sweet, innocent Perrie, took him on the ride of his life.

All the Perries he had seen flashed behind his eyes—the gentle mother, the laughing storyteller, the small tiger who'd defended her cub. But above him now, Mitch saw a different woman, a small Valkyrie filled with courage and fire and a smoldering sensuality that sucked the breath from his lungs.

Eyes closed, head thrown back, golden hair swaying over plump breasts and flaring nipples, she was a goddess, a woman of many faces, a Scheherazade to beguile a man's senses.

Perrie opened her eyes, her body alive with the feel of him inside her, her skin rippling with gooseflesh from the glory of his touch, and looked down into eyes gone dark chocolate, velvety-soft yet burning with challenge.

"Mitch, I don't—I want—"

He seemed to understand, reversing their positions in one swift move, rising above her like some pagan god. His strokes went deeper yet, and Perrie gasped.

He stilled for one moment, and their eyes met. And in that instant, the presence of something momentous rose between them...wrapped around them...called out to some hidden part of each one.

For an endless span, they barely breathed. In Mitch's eyes, Perrie saw something flicker, like he felt it, too, this longing she couldn't define.

It was too much, too frightening. Seeking oblivion instead, she pulled him closer, winding her legs around his hips. Sensing the pull of that elusive heaven he'd shown her before, but wanting something else, too—something more.

He shook his head as if denying the draw. He drove into her, closing his eyes, his face once again a mask. Alone again as she'd seen him so often.

And then Perrie realized what it was she wanted. Love. To give this man love.

Her thoughts scrambled in confusion. She wanted to retreat, to run away from what she was feeling, from such a foolish, unattainable need.

But before she could make sense of any of it, Mitch bent his head and took her mouth in imitation of the strokes inside her body. He surrounded her, filled her, cast away anything inside her but himself. She was lost in the wonder of Mitch, only Mitch, when the wonder exploded and the world went white behind her eyes. He took her soaring out beyond anything she'd ever sensed, ever felt, ever known.

Mitch felt it, too, and in the midst of ecstasy, he knew a dread so deep it seared his soul.

All of this, all that he felt, all that burst inside him now would vanish. He would be as he had always been. Alone.

And once again he would know the bitter sting of what he had lost.

Mitch fought to hold back, not to feel anymore. She would tear out his heart. He would not survive.

But she was too warm, too willing, too sweet. Like a sorceress she called forth all that he claimed as his own.

Mitch fought the pull, but it was too strong. He yearned for an end to his darkness, a sweet taste of peace. Like it or not, Perrie had shown him both, and the need of even a taste brought him to his knees.

With a groan that tore at the very roots of his soul, Mitch surrendered. With one last, bittersweet thrust, Mitch sent them spiraling, holding her tightly against him while they careened through a sky shot with sparks, whirling with color, sizzling with a fire that had surely branded him to his depths.

But even as she pulsed around him, sanity battered at euphoria. With a sudden, awful clarity, he realized that he'd surrendered too soon, that something was missing.

He could sink into her body a thousand times and

he would never find what he needed most, wanted most. She could share her body with him, but she kept the secrets of her heart to herself. Warming himself at her gentle fire, feeling a moment of peace, was not enough.

He'd been alone for so long. He'd never known how it could feel to be this close. She'd taunted him with this taste, but still she held back, even after what they'd shared. He had to have more.

"Perrie," he whispered, rolling to his side, pulling her near, his breath warm and soft against her temple. "Tell me what's wrong. Tell me why you wouldn't come to Cy. Tell me why you're afraid."

She went stiff in his arms, as though the moments just past had been a dream. "There's nothing wrong."

But she was lying—he could hear it in her voice, feel it in her frame. He should let it go, make love to her again. Settle for what he could have, and forget what she held back.

But he could not. "Let me help. This woman in my arms is not the woman who wouldn't come to the phone when Cy was dying. Explain it to me. Tell me what's wrong."

If he'd thought her body stiff before, it was rigid now. She pulled away and sat up, the curtain of her hair hiding her face. "I was—traveling. I told you. I didn't know."

"You're lying." He sat up, too, turning her to face him, pushing back her hair, gripping her jaw. "Look at me and tell me that again."

Blue eyes darkened, and she swallowed hard. He saw the briefest flicker, but it could have been the fire's light.

"I was out of the country. No one told me you called." Her voice was stronger, but it didn't matter. Her eyes told the truth. Despite what they'd shared, she still did not trust him.

He swore under his breath, and Perrie jerked away as if he'd struck her. She rose to her feet, holding her clothes in front of her like a shield.

Her voice shook slightly when she spoke. "This was a mistake. I'm sorry. I was just—you saved Davey and I—"

If she'd cut his heart out with a rusty knife, it couldn't have hurt any more. A debt. She was only paying a debt. She didn't trust him enough to tell him the truth about her past, and she had only lain with him because he'd saved her son.

At sixteen, he'd learned the price of letting his emotions run free. He'd never made that mistake again—until now. He'd let himself feel too much ever since they'd come, been lulled into thinking nothing would happen that he couldn't control.

But tonight, tonight was deadly. He'd opened the lamp and let the genie out for moments of beauty so sublime he knew he'd feel the loss for the rest of his life. He'd unleashed passions and let down his guard—and now the genie didn't want to go back into the lamp.

Staring at the woman who had turned his soul inside out and then dropped it on the ground like so much trash, Mitch couldn't believe he'd been such a fool. Jerking on his jeans, he scooped the rest of his clothes up off the floor, shoving away pain sharp as a dagger sliding into an unprotected chest.

He had to get away. Before it was too late.

"You're right," he said. "It won't happen again."

He left the room.

Perrie watched him go, knowing a grief so keen she didn't know how she would bear it. Wanting to call him back, wanting to explain. But she couldn't falter now.

He would never know it, but she did this for him. Tearing out her heart with bare hands would hurt less. Her body still hummed from the splendor of his loving, yet her mouth tasted only of ashes.

When she heard the door to his room click shut, she sank to the floor and buried her face in her hands.

And silently wept.

Chapter Eleven

When Perrie awoke, the sun was high overhead. She and Davey were alone.

In the bright light of day, it all seemed a dream— but the memories were too sharp, too pungent.

Too painful.

She could still feel Mitch inside her, still see him rising above her like a warrior god. Still feel the earth-shattering power of her release, the sense of safety in his arms.

The sense of heaven found…and paradise lost.

He had offered his help—and she had answered him with lies. She didn't know which of them she had hurt worse.

Perrie shot out of bed to escape the guilt that

pounded away at her. Padding into the kitchen, she saw his dark scrawl on the scrap of paper.

"Gone to town for supplies." He hadn't wanted to see her after last night. His metamorphosis from generous, breathtaking lover back to closed-in loner had been heartbreaking to watch.

Because she knew it was squarely her fault.

She knew how alone he was, had seen how hard trust came to him, yet when it came time to answer his trust, she had not. She had wanted to—oh, how she had wanted to spill out her story, to accept his strength…his aid and comfort.

But he deserved better.

She'd seen what Simon could do to anyone who got in his way. Mitch was big and strong, but Simon had a hundred men at his back. And Simon had something else Mitch did not—enough cruelty and ruthlessness for a thousand.

So no matter how much she wanted to ask for Mitch's help, she could not. He had earned better repayment for all he'd done for her and her son.

Whatever had happened in his life to make him close down like he had, it must have been very bad. What she could bring to his doorstep would be worse. For the sake of his kindness to her, for his gentle care of her child, for the life he had saved…and for showing her the woman she could be, she would not yield to the temptation to lay her troubles on his shoulders, no matter how broad.

They had to leave. Today, while he was gone. She would keep heading west, and they must depart before the next snow came. Before she spent any more time with Mitch and let her heart take the lead.

Perrie walked back into the bedroom. "Wake up, Davey." She touched his shoulder gently. "Rise and shine, sleepyhead."

Trusting blue eyes opened slowly, lit from within. "I'm still sleepy." He yawned.

"How do you feel, sweetie?"

His eyes popped open, and he sat up, a little less agile than normal. "Ow—sore." His head swiveled toward the door. "Where's Mitch? I gotta ask him something."

"He's not here."

Davey's shoulders sagged. "I wanted to go out in the woods with him today. I thought he could show me how he climbed that cliff."

Perrie resisted the urge to roll her eyes at his obviously intact sense of adventure, grateful for anything to stem the ache in her heart. "I don't think you need to be doing anything like that for a while."

"Mitch would take care of me. When he gets back, I'll ask him if we can do it tomorrow."

This wouldn't be easy. "Sweetheart, we can't stay here, now that Grandpa Cy is gone."

His gaze was clear and trusting. "Sure we can. Mitch likes us."

"Well, yes, Mitch is very fond of you, but he won't be staying, either. He has jobs waiting for him. He has to travel a lot."

Davey frowned faintly. "Then we should go with him."

"I'm afraid that's not possible. It would interfere with his work."

"But we could stay here and wait for him, right? He could come home when he was finished?"

The love he bore Mitch shone from his innocent gaze. Perrie's chest tightened. "Davey, you and I aren't really the right people to stay here through a whole winter when all it does is snow. Besides, once we get settled, you can have a yard and meet some friends and even watch cartoons again. You'd like that, wouldn't you?"

Davey shook his head. "Mitch was right. TV's not such a big deal."

This was not the time for his stubborn streak to rear its head. "Davey, we can't stay here. We have to pack and leave while we still have enough sun to make it to the car."

"You mean today? We have to leave today?" He looked horrified.

"Yes, sweetheart. Now, up and at 'em. You get dressed, and I'll fix us something to eat."

"What about Mitch? I need to talk to him." The pouting lower lip had made way for a sense of urgency on his face.

"We'll write Mitch once we get to our new town, and maybe he'll come to visit." Perhaps it could happen that way, though not anytime soon.

"We can't just leave without saying goodbye."

"David Lee Matheson, don't argue with me."

Why did this have to be so hard? But she couldn't explain, not to a five-year-old.

He looked so forlorn, so unsettled. The air whooshed from her chest. Dropping to a crouch, she held his shoulders. "Davey, Mitch has been very good to you—to both of us. There are grown-up reasons why this is the best thing to do for Mitch, and I have to ask you to trust me on this. We have to leave today, and I need you to help me. I know you care about Mitch. I care about him, too, and that's why we have to go. He is too kind to us to tell us to leave, but he's not used to living with other people. We came up here to live with Grandpa Cy, but Grandpa's gone. This is Mitch's cabin now—"

"He would let us stay. I know he would."

Not after last night, she thought. *Not after what I did.*

"Sweetie, he likes living alone. It's what he's used to. And he needs freedom to travel and not worry about us. I know it's hard to leave Mitch, but sometimes you have to do the hard things for the sake of someone you care about. If you care about him—"

"I love Mitch—" Davey interjected, blue eyes filling with tears.

She nodded, drawing him close. "I know you do. So we have to do the right thing and leave now, so he can go on with his life."

He burst into broken sobs against her neck. Perrie rubbed his back, fighting back her own despair.

They had to do this. There was little she could do to repay Mitch's kindness, but she could do this for him.

Straightening her shoulders and lifting her head, she pulled Davey out in front of her. "If ever there was a time to be grown-up, Davey, this is it. Now please help me." But rebellion still stirred within the heartbreak in his eyes. She made one more effort. "We'll leave Mitch a note, one from you in which you can tell me what to say and I'll write it—"

"I can write my own name and his, too." Davey's jaw jutted. They were far from through with this, she could tell.

"Fine. Then you write those, and tell me what you want written in the middle. We'll leave the notes, and when we're settled, we'll let him know where we are." It wasn't quite a lie. Perhaps her letter to the reporter would bear fruit, and Simon would be caught one day soon. Then she would get back her life. And maybe contact Mitch.

But looking at Davey, she could tell that this was one of the times when her will would just have to prevail. Rising to her feet, she steeled herself. "Please dress warmly in the clothes I've set out. I'll fix us something to eat." Then she left the room, knowing she hadn't crossed the last hurdle.

But more sure than ever that this was the right thing to do. Davey would only get more attached if they stayed.

* * *

Mitch entered the general store, mentally assembling the list of supplies he would need to take to Perrie and Davey, unease a hard knot in his gut at the thought of leaving them there through the winter.

But he would leave. After last night, one of them had to go. Cy might have given him the cabin, but it had only been because Perrie had vanished from Cy's life. Mitch was convinced that something had kept her from being there for her grandfather. The old man would have wanted her to have the only thing he'd had to hand down.

Perrie knew how to handle herself up there. Her strength was almost fully returned. He would make sure there was a winter's supply of wood and plenty of supplies. He would ask Hank Pearson at the ranger station to check in on them often.

Maybe he could come back and check himself—

No. Not a good idea, but it was hard as hell to think of leaving them there. What other choice existed? He couldn't stay there and not want her. The last days had seduced him, made him wish for a dream. He'd let his damn fool heart open, let longing inside. Let himself pretend that the haven was real.

But it wasn't. Only the imaginings of a heart too long unused. He had to get out before there was nothing left of him to save. Rebuilding from scratch again might be more than he could bear. He had to lock the gates now.

"Hey, Mitch, how ya doin'?" Curly Bondurant

greeted him from behind the cash register. "Didn't expect to see you back so soon. Get much snow up there?"

"Enough," he answered. "Already melting, though."

"Yeah, might have a decent break before the next one. Here to stock up a little more?"

Mitch nodded.

"Don't know how you stand it, no power or phone up there. Betty would go crazy without her TV or folks to talk to."

He'd been alone so long, it had come to seem normal. It was his life. At least until Perrie and her child—

No. He couldn't think about how it would feel without them. It was what it was. What had to be. Shaking his head, Mitch headed for the shelves of canned goods, looking for those noodle things Davey had said he liked.

"Say, Mitch, almost forgot." Curly walked over and handed him two envelopes. "You got some mail. A letter for you and another one addressed to someone named Matheson sent in care of Cy. You got company up there?"

"Thanks." But he didn't answer Curly, studying the envelope addressed to Perrie. A Boston postmark. Mentally shrugging, he stuck it in his pocket, then looked at the one addressed to him. His heart thumped once, hard.

From Texas. From Morning Star.

Mitch's stomach rose, then plummeted. He didn't

recognize the bold scrawl forming his name. It wasn't his father's handwriting—at least, he didn't think so. He hadn't seen it in years.

He couldn't decide whether to stuff it in his pocket, too, or go ahead and read it. Finally, curiosity won out. He turned toward the door. "I'll be back."

Curly was obviously curious. "No need to go outside to read it. Good light in here."

Mitch didn't spare him a look, just kept walking. Curly's need for entertainment wasn't his concern.

Outside, he leaned against his truck, holding the envelope in his hands, a jumble of feelings tossing inside him. A letter from home, or someone close. But Morning Star hadn't been home for half his life now.

His gut told him this wasn't good news. He wondered how anyone had found him here.

Finally, he knew he had to read it, whatever it said. Tearing open the flap, he pulled out two sheets of paper inside.

Dear Mitch,

It's been a long time, but I want you to come home.

Home. The word sank in his chest like a stone tumbling over a cliff. Flashes of memory: his mother dying in his arms, his father's rage as he told Mitch never to come back—

Mitch flipped to the last page, to the signature.

"Boone." His brother had been fourteen, raw-boned and all feet, just getting his height the last time Mitch had seen him. How did he look now? And why did Boone want him to come back?

Longing, swift and sharp, sank claws in his heart. He turned back to the first page.

I don't know how to say it easy, so I'll just say it. Dad is dead. His heart gave out. He left the ranch to you and me and Maddie.

Sam was dead. Mitch couldn't take it in. The father he had once worshiped...who had banished him forever. Dead. They would never reconcile, never take back the hateful words between them.

Mitch stared out across the road, seeing nothing. And wanted to howl.

He tightened his jaw. Dead was dead. Nothing he could do now. He turned back to the letter, finally noticing the other name.

Maddie? Who was Maddie?

Maddie's my wife. It's a long story, but she's Dalton Wheeler's daughter.

Dalton Wheeler? The one who had vanished years ago? The ranch had been the old Wheeler place until Dalton's mother died back when Mitch and Boone were kids.

Boone. Married. Mitch couldn't get the picture of a gangly fourteen-year-old out of his head.

You'll like her, Mitch. And we have a lot
to talk about. Dad hired a private investigator
to look for you and me both, but you're one
hard guy to find.

Why had Sam needed to hunt for Boone? As
much as Boone had loved the old place, Mitch had
always assumed he would stay and take over one
day.

And there's more. We've got a half sister
we never knew about. Long story, but we're
looking for her now.

Mitch leaned heavily against his truck. A half
sister? Had Sam cheated on their mother?

He closed his sagging jaw. Hell of a deal, dropping only part of a bombshell like that. Boone
hadn't changed much—still knew how to taunt his
older brother.

Mitch shook his head and read on.

I'm giving you a chance to come back by
yourself, but I'll warn you—I'm coming after
you if you don't show up pretty soon. Dad was
wrong to do what he did, and in the end, he
knew it. I want my brother back. You belong
on this land, same as I do.

You never should have had to leave. Mad-
die's made this place feel like it did when
Mom was alive, but there's one thing missing.
You.

Mitch bowed his head. Jenny would have still been there, making it a happy place, if it hadn't been for him. He couldn't go back. It was his fault that everything had gone wrong.

This is your home, Mitch, and you've got family waiting. It's been too long. Besides, I need to show you I can take you now.

Mitch snorted, and a laugh almost broke through. *You and whose army, little brother?* Then he read the last line and sobered again.

I've missed you, big brother. Come on back where you belong.

Boone

Mitch's chest ached with a pain sharper than any he'd felt since the night his mother died. *Home.* Hadn't he wanted to go there a million times? Hadn't it been like cutting his heart out to have to leave, knowing he could never return?

Damn you, Sam Gallagher. Why did you die on me? We can't ever fix it now.

And damn me, for starting the whole nightmare.

Too much was kicking up inside him. He didn't want to leave the one place that was starting to feel like home. He didn't know how to go back to the home he had lost. And the last thing Mitch wanted to do was to walk back in that store and think about groceries.

Which was why that's exactly what he'd do.

Shoving the letter in his pocket, Mitch squared his shoulders and headed back into the store.

Pulling on the homemade travois Cy had fashioned, Mitch pulled the heavy load through the woods, the cabin's contours visible now. The long drive had done nothing to settle the turmoil inside him.

The last person he wanted to see right now was Perrie. Or Davey. They made him feel too much, and feelings had always been the enemy. Always would be. From the day he'd fought with his father and taken off in a rage, life had pounded that lesson into him again and again.

Don't feel. Just put one foot in front of the other. If he hurried, there was a slim chance he could pack up and leave before nightfall. He just had to get through the next couple of hours, and then he could be alone again. Put his careening thoughts in order.

At the cabin steps, he dropped the harness of the travois. Drawing a deep breath, he steeled himself to enter.

The first thing he saw when he did enter was their suitcases, stacked by the door.

Perrie walked into the room, her hands full of Davey's toys. When she saw him, she froze.

"What's this?" he asked.

"We're leaving."

If he'd had any lingering notion that last night had meant anything to her, this put Paid to it. "Where are you going?"

"It's not your concern." But she wouldn't look at him, her movements jerky, almost feverish as she set the toys on the sofa and began to stuff them into the waiting bags.

"Do you even know where you're going?"

"It's not your concern." Her voice quavered just a bit.

"You don't, do you?" When she still didn't answer, the upheaval inside him at last had a target. "What the hell are you doing? What kind of mother are you that you'd just take off with that boy, not knowing where you're headed?"

She shrank from his words like he'd landed punches, but the pressure inside him was too intense, too primed to blow.

But she still didn't answer.

"What if you get sick again, huh? Do you even have any money to take care of him? And what about that junky damn car you're driving? What if it breaks down? Are you so desperate to get away from me that you'll risk your child's life?"

He stalked across the floor, looming over her. "What are you running from, Perrie?"

Her head jerked up in surprise.

"It's Davey's father, isn't it?"

All color drained from her face. "You—you don't—you can't know that."

"But it's true, isn't it? You're on the run. Tell me why. Tell me what he's done to you."

She shook her head sharply and turned back to her packing. "It's not your problem."

"It is when you're irresponsible enough to endanger that boy. I won't let you do it."

"You can't stop me."

"I damn well can, and I will if you don't start thinking of your boy instead of yourself!"

"I am thinking of him—" she shouted. "That's why I have to go." She stalked to the door and jerked it open. "Davey! Come on, time to go now."

Mitch grabbed the door out of her hands, slamming it shut. "You are not taking off like this."

"I have to." Her chin tilted stubbornly, her eyes sparking.

"You don't have to. I'm leaving. Tonight."

Her eyes widened. "This is your place. You don't have to go. It's not right." She pulled the door open again. "Davey, come in right this minute. I know you're mad, but answer me right now."

"Why is he mad?"

She shot him an accusing glare. "Because he doesn't want to leave you."

Something fast and fierce warmed Mitch's heart. He would miss the boy, too. And he would be the one to go, not them. But before he left, he would grant himself one last pleasure. He would hold the boy once more, as he could never again hold the boy's mother.

Perrie reached for her coat, muttering. "That

child's stubborn streak is going to be the death of me, I swear.''

Mitch stopped her with one hand on her arm. ''Let me, all right? Maybe he'll come to me. Let me talk to him a minute.''

Perrie studied him, and within her eyes he saw the faintest flicker that made him want—

Never mind. Pushing past her, he went outside, calling the boy who had walked into his life and stolen a big piece of an old rusty heart.

Perrie looked around her when he left, trying to see this place as her new home. It was so tempting, and Mitch had hit at her sore point. She *was* afraid of taking off with Davey, afraid that she couldn't hide him well enough, couldn't make the life he deserved. But she couldn't rob Mitch of the only home he had. And she couldn't forget the threat of Simon. Mitch hadn't asked for that. But maybe—

The door burst open. ''He's not around here, unless he's just not answering me. Would he have run off?'' Mitch asked.

Fear shoved away Perrie's first flood of anger. Would he have run away? Was he that upset about leaving?

''I don't know. He's never done anything like that before, but he was dead-set on seeing you again. Maybe he's just hiding.''

''If he wanted to see me, why won't he answer?''

A big fist squeezed the air from her lungs. ''Oh,

God. Simon,'' she whispered. What if Simon had him?

"What did you say?"

But she barely heard him. Either Simon had found them or Davey was all alone out in the wilderness. All she could think of was the cliff, the bears, all the places around here for him to get hurt—

Mitch reached her side and pulled her into his chest. "Stop. We'll find him. I can track anything. The snow is melting, but he'll still make easy prints." His voice sounded absolutely certain.

"I'm coming with you." She pulled away.

He held on to her arms, studying her face. Then he nodded. "All right, but you'll have to keep up. It'll be dark soon and the temperatures will drop fast."

"I'll keep up." Thoughts of her child alone, freezing in the darkness, much less all the other things that could—

"Stop letting your imagination run wild. You need to stay alert, and you can't do that if your emotions are getting the better of you."

She could see his face forming into its customary mask. Was this how he'd lived his whole life?

Perrie pulled on her outer gear and dumped out a backpack, placing two blankets inside. Mitch turned away and gathered up his own supplies.

"You ready?" His face was grim, set into lines of sheer determination. The sight of it lifted her spirits. If anyone could find her son, it was Mitch.

She wouldn't let herself think of the alternative.

"Stay behind me, and don't talk unless it's urgent."

Perrie nodded.

"We'll find him. I promise you that."

"I believe you," she said softly.

Mitch's eyes softened. For a moment he looked like he wanted to say something else.

And Perrie wanted to hear it.

Then he shook his head and opened the door. Perrie followed behind him.

Dusk was gathering, and they hadn't yet found him. The mushy snow had washed away Davey's trail in several places, costing Mitch precious time before he would lose the light. Mitch shut his mind to all the horrors he knew were running through Perrie's brain. A cold mind was essential. Emotion only obscured thinking.

He stopped, dead still, then reached down to pick up an object, his heart both sinking and rising fast. He turned and held it out to Perrie.

"Oh, no," she gasped. "Davey's bear." Her gaze shot up to his. "He would never let this go if he—"

Mitch grasped her arm, pulled her into his chest. "Stop thinking the worst, Perrie. It's a good sign. Explains why his tracks have been circling so oddly the last few yards. He must have dropped it and spent time looking for it. The tracks are fresh."

"Davey!" she called out, her voice ringing off the mountainside. "Where are you?"

No answer. "Let me," he said. He called out, too, but only silence met them.

"Oh, Mitch, it's getting darker by the minute."

"Which is why we have to keep looking. Come on."

Blanking his mind to anything but the trail, Mitch studied the rocks, the bushes and the ground. Finally, one trail branched off from the maze of tracks near the wooden bear. With long strides, Mitch followed it, reaching back for Perrie's hand to pull her along.

Finally he saw it. And blessed Perrie for buying the boy a bright red coat. But the mound of red wasn't moving, and Mitch's heart leapt to his throat.

He wished he could make Perrie stay back until he took a look. If something had happened—

He never wanted Perrie to have to live, night after night, with the sight branded into her brain like the vision he had in his, of his mother, blond hair running red with blood—

"Stay here," he ordered.

"What?"

"Let me look first."

"Wha—oh, God—" She took off running.

Mitch passed her, reaching Davey first and using his body to shield her from the sight.

He could barely feel her hands clawing at his shoulder, too lost in the thumping of his heart, the pounding rush of blood in his veins as he turned Davey over—

Blue eyes opened slowly. And smiled sleepily. "Mitch!"

For the rest of his life, Mitch would take all the bad luck fate wanted to sling his way, as payment for the joy shooting through his veins now. He pulled Davey up into his arms and brought Perrie around, including her, too. For a moment, the three of them clung, like shipwreck survivors.

The tree before Mitch blurred. He couldn't find his voice to ask the routine questions.

Perrie pulled away and asked them first. "Are you hurt?" Frantically she felt over her child's head, his limbs, his torso.

Davey looked groggy and confused. "I was just asleep. I got so tired and I couldn't figure out how to get back, so I decided to rest for a minute—" His face fell. "I lost my bear, Mitch," he whispered. "And Mom says we have to leave, and there's no time for you to make me another one. I'm so sorry—" Tears formed in his eyes, and he threw himself back into Mitch's arms.

"I don't want to leave you. I thought if I hid in the woods, you would have time to come back and you could help me convince Mom that we should stay." Davey pulled away, his small hands framing Mitch's face. "I wish you could be my dad, Mitch. I don't want to go. Tell Mom we can stay— please."

If someone had slammed a two-by-four against his head, Mitch couldn't feel more disoriented.

Perrie gasped and reached for her son. "Sweetie, don't say that. You can't just ask Mitch to be your father."

"Why not?"

Why not, indeed? Mitch's mind whirled. The boy's words ricocheted around in his head, rocketing past the adrenaline rush and all the emotions he'd felt when he'd thought the boy was—

Mitch didn't know what to say. Or feel. *Davey's dad.* He closed his eyes. Oh, God. How fine that would be.

If only Davey's mother wanted him, too.

Perrie watched him struggle. When he didn't answer Davey, a cold ball lodged in her chest.

She took refuge in action. "Let's get you back to the cabin. We—that is, I—" Her eyes stung.

Then she got mad. "You scared us to death, young man," she scolded. "Don't you ever—" Her voice broke, and she turned away.

"You promised me you wouldn't wander off by yourself," Mitch reminded the boy. "If a man's word is no good, then he can't call himself a man."

Davey's lower lip trembled. "I didn't mean to get lost."

Mitch didn't relent. "You still left without telling anyone where you were going."

Her son's voice grew smaller. "I'm sorry, Mitch."

"Your mom is the one who deserves your apology. She takes good care of you, and this is a poor way to treat someone who loves you.''

''I'm sorry, Mom. I just really, really didn't want to leave Mitch. Do we still have to go?''

Her hand trembled as she reached out to stroke his head, wishing she could spare him. ''Davey, we can't just—'' Her shoulders sagged. ''There's too much you don't understand.''

''We can't leave tonight, right?'' His blue eyes filled with hope. ''It's almost dark.''

No, it would be foolish in the extreme. But Mitch's silence shouted out how much he wished for them to be gone. She'd dared to hope, for that shining moment when he'd held them both so close, that he wanted…more.

His face impassive, Mitch leaned down and picked up Davey. ''Give me your hand.''

Without hesitation, Davey stretched out his fingers, the trust in his eyes quick and easily given. How much leaving would hurt her child.

Mitch placed Davey's bear in his palm.

''You found my bear!'' Davey crowed. Then he frowned faintly. ''He's kinda dirty. Is he ruined?''

''Nah,'' Mitch answered. ''It gives him character.''

''What's character, Mom?''

''I—'' She looked at Mitch, but his gaze was shuttered. She had no idea what he was thinking. And she was so drained. ''Not now, sweetheart.'' She turned, desperate to get away.

With Davey perched on one arm, Mitch wrapped

the other around her stiff shoulders. In some ways it was more cruel than anything he'd ever done, but she couldn't think about it, not now. She had to stay busy, try not to think.

They would head back to the cabin, then get warm and eat something, and put Davey to bed.

And in the morning it would all be over.

Chapter Twelve

Mitch walked back toward the fireplace from the bedroom, Davey's whispered words echoing in his head.

I love you, Mitch.

How long since he'd heard those words from another living being?

He knew, down to the minute.

The night his mother died. In his arms. Because of him.

A lifetime had passed since that night. Years filled first with rage, with blind, stumbling steps to find some way to kill the pain.

Then Cy had come along and pulled him up by the scruff of his neck, a surly old man who'd given

Mitch the closest thing he'd had to affection since he'd left Morning Star.

He'd told himself that he'd found the answer, that not feeling was the key. Years had passed, years in which Mitch's detachment grew by the day, until he'd perfected a shell so thick it couldn't be pierced.

Until he'd met a blue-eyed angel...and held her child in his arms. And his shell had developed cracks.

He didn't know how the woman and child had slipped inside, only that they had. And that it hurt like hell to feel again.

Now Perrie wanted to leave, her lies intact. Just walk away as though he could simply forget them. As though last night had never happened.

Maybe for her it had been nothing. But not for him.

He shouldn't care—after all, it was what he'd wanted since the day they'd met. For her to get out of his life, to let him go back to the solitude that was what he knew best.

But she would tell him what he needed to know first. And then he would decide—

What? He had no claim on them, wanted none.

He heard her last good-night to Davey, then the soft click as she closed the bedroom door.

And then he felt her presence like the rays of the rising sun.

Mitch turned, and Perrie resisted the urge to run.

She felt the air between them thicken, a broth

boiling over with too much unsaid, too much unexplained. Her nerves still vibrated with the remnants of terror that Simon had somehow found Davey. She had seen straight into the heart of her inability to truly protect her son. The last two days had provided ample proof of what Simon had always said, that she was only a pretty ornament, good for little else.

Deep within her, resentment raged. She kicked at fate's shins, fought battles with her fears.

I am not useless. I will not give in. Simon is wrong, and I will defeat him.

But between every word shot images that called her a fool. Davey on the ledge, inches from death. Davey lost in a frozen wilderness.

Mitch, strong and fierce, protecting them at every turn.

He was so powerful. She was so afraid.

And the knowledge made her furious, as much at him as at herself. He'd made his wishes clear by his silence as much as his words.

He wanted to be alone. Perrie picked up a toy and stared blindly at the suitcase she'd left open.

"What did Simon do to you?"

Mitch's question zeroed in too close. "Nothing," she shot back, turning to pack.

He crossed the floor in two long strides, whirling her back to face him. "This stops now, Perrie. I've listened to all the lies I'm going to tolerate from you."

She saw red. "You don't have to tolerate anything. I'm leaving, first thing in the morning. We won't be your concern anymore.''

His nostrils flared; his gaze narrowed. ''Someone needs to be concerned about you. You're acting like an irresponsible fool.''

Perrie shoved away from him, suddenly unable to breathe for the thick swirl of emotions clogging the air. ''You don't know what you're talking about.''

''Then tell me. Why are you running? What has he done to you? Why are you afraid?''

Mitch watched the war go on inside her, watched her defenses go up, her arms crossing over her chest, hugging her damn secrets closer than ever. He wanted to grab her, to shake loose the truth that stood between them.

He wanted to hold her, to tell her that he would protect her forever. That he'd be the prince who would ride to her rescue.

But he couldn't do that. He didn't know the first thing about love. He was alone, and that was how it had to be. Too many people he loved had suffered before. He didn't want to feel anything, damn it. Why wouldn't she leave him in peace?

Why couldn't he forget? Just let them go?

He couldn't need her. Couldn't let her widen the cracks.

But it was too late. She already had.

The tempest inside him boiled higher. Mitch had to get out of here before he lost the last hope of control. Outside. They needed more wood.

Whirling away, he grabbed for his coat, and a white scrap fell out of his pocket.

The letter. Perrie's letter.

He leaned down and picked it off the floor, holding it out to her. "Here—this came for you."

Perrie shook her head and looked at it like it was poison. "For me?"

"Yeah—came general delivery. I stuck it in my pocket and forgot about it when Davey—" He shoved it at her again.

For the longest time she stood there, emotions chasing across her face. Finally she reached out slowly and took it. She didn't open it, simply stared at the writing on the front.

Then, like she was waking from a dream, she slit it open, pulled out the paper inside and read.

And went pale as a ghost, swaying on her feet.

Mitch crossed to her quickly. "What is it?"

Perrie shook her head and stepped away, staring into the fire, the letter dangling from her hand.

"What's wrong? Damn it, Perrie, answer me."

Mutely she handed him the letter. Mitch took it and scanned the contents quickly.

Perrie—

Your letter worked. Mr. Matheson has been indicted. The district attorney needs to talk to you to make their case. It's your chance to put him away for a good long time. If you don't,

he'll walk and you'll never be free of him.
　Come back to Boston and finish this.

　　　　　　　　　　　　　　Your friend,
　　　　　　　　　　　　　　Elias

"Who's Elias?" he asked.

"My ex-husband's gardener."

"What does he mean, your letter worked? What's the indictment about?"

Perrie couldn't face him, her mind locking down. *Go back to Boston. Into the serpent's den.*

She couldn't do it. Couldn't take Davey back into Simon's reach.

But if she didn't, she'd never be free.

"Come on, Perrie, trust me."

Oh, how she wanted to do that, wanted his help in sorting out what she should do. Her thoughts tumbled over one another as she searched for an answer.

"Simon—" She choked on her explanation. How could Mitch possibly understand what a fool she'd been? How weak not to break away years before?

You can break away now, Perrie. Take one step and tell Mitch.

But he would despise her for being a coward. Such a strong man could never understand.

She wanted to tell him—badly. But how could she drag him into this?

"I have to leave, Mitch."

"To testify?"

"I can't." Her chest felt tight. "I—"

"Why not?"

She looked up at him, whispering her disgrace. "I'm afraid to go back."

"Why? What's he done?"

"What hasn't he done?" She choked out a laugh. "My ex-husband is a very rich man, but his family's wealth was never enough. He wanted more. He's laundered money for drug dealers, he's been involved in gambling—I don't know all that he's done."

She whirled. "Except that when I first tried to break out of the prison he'd built around me, the bodyguard who helped me mysteriously turned up dead. I can't prove that he murdered Billy, but I know he did."

"Prison?" His eyes went dark and angry. "What do you mean?"

Perrie looked at the floor. "I'm ashamed to tell you."

"Why should you be ashamed? You were the victim."

Her head jerked up. "I was weak. So blinded by the glamorous lifestyle he promised that I didn't see until it was too late that I was a thing to him, another pretty object to be admired when he wanted and put on the shelf in between—and never, ever to be shared with anyone else."

"You were young. You didn't know."

She laughed and began to pace. "But I didn't stay young. I just stayed scared. He would make me—" The words choked her throat. "He liked to play these games in the bedroom—"

Mitch grasped her arm and turned her around, pulling her into his hard chest. "Don't—you don't have to tell me." One big hand stroked her hair.

Perrie leaned into the safety of his arms. "Until last night," she whispered. "I never knew—I've never experienced what you made me feel."

Mitch tightened his arms around her, her pain touching him as if it were his own. Her story explained a lot of things. "It wasn't your fault."

Her head jerked back, her eyes sparking, filling with angry tears. "I tried to escape, but he found me and brought me back." Her gaze dropped. "He beat me and raped me, locked me up tighter than ever. And then Davey was born and—"

Dear God, Mitch thought. Davey was the result of the rape. "It doesn't matter. Davey's nothing like him. You've done a great job with him."

"I brought a child into that life," she flared.

"You had no choice. And you obviously protected him. There's not a thing wrong with him."

"I thought we were finished with Simon. He didn't believe Davey was his, thought the bodyguard and I—" Her voice faded. But then she straightened. "Then he found a woman he wanted to marry, and I thought we'd been set free."

Her gaze met his again. "He divorced me, gave me some money I put away for Davey. The only condition was that I couldn't take Davey from Boston. The Mathesons are very powerful, and Simon told me he would take Davey away if I tried, even though he cared nothing about him. Just pride of ownership, like with me. I was so happy to be away, so happy that he was out of our lives. Everything was good for a while, and then—'' Her voice broke.

Mitch fought against his rage, simply holding her close, waiting for the rest.

"Then he found out his new wife couldn't bear children. He decided that he'd claim Davey, no matter his private doubts. I had figured out some things by then, things about how he made his money. I threatened to go to the police if he didn't leave Davey alone.

"He just laughed. Asked me why anyone would believe me over him. Told me he had all kinds of evidence to prove I was an unfit mother. He said if I ever breathed a word, he'd take Davey away and I'd never see him again."

Mitch knew how fierce her love was for her child. He could feel how afraid she was. He wanted to kill Matheson himself.

"And then he decided to teach me a lesson. He picked Davey up from school one afternoon and took him away for two days. The police wouldn't help me. I had no idea where he was. I was out of my mind with fear.

"When he brought him back, Davey was a different child. Frightened and too quiet. I knew then that I was out of options. I had to run. Elias helped me, but before I left, I wrote down everything I knew and Elias sent it to the top investigative reporter in Boston."

She met his gaze. "And then I headed here, to Grandpa Cy. I knew he wouldn't turn me away, even though I hadn't heard from him in years. I was just grateful that I'd never told Simon about him and Simon wouldn't know to look here for us."

Blue eyes pleaded with him. "I truly didn't know Grandpa was sick, Mitch. I would never have turned away from him."

Mitch nodded. "I believe you." He stroked her face. "Why wouldn't you tell me all this before?" Though he knew. He'd held her in contempt, made it clear she was unwelcome.

But her answer shocked him. "You don't know what he's like. Simon would hurt you, too, if he came here and found that you had helped us."

Mitch couldn't take it in. She was protecting him? "I've been taking care of myself since I was sixteen, Perrie. He can't hurt me."

"He's evil, Mitch. Evil to the bone. He's not just mean, but there's something twisted inside him. He'd do anything to get us back—anything."

"That's why you have to go back and testify."

She jerked away from him, agitation in every line of her frame. "You don't know what you're asking."

"Perrie, you have to face this or you and Davey have no future. You can't keep running away."

Perrie laughed bitterly and whirled to face him. "You're a fine one to be talking." She stabbed a finger in his direction. "What are you doing here, if not hiding out? You won't let anyone close, won't stay in one place. Something's happened in your life and you're still running away from it— who are you to tell me I have to face Simon?''

Mitch took a step back from her anger, fury shooting high in his veins. He clenched his fists, ready to turn and—

And walk away. Just like she'd accused.

How different was that from Perrie running?

Within him boiled a potent brew of too many feelings he couldn't contain. He grasped at a lifetime of rigid control, knowing that like a pressure cooker over a fire turned too high, too much threatened to blow free. Hadn't he learned the price of emotion careening around, destroying everything in its path?

Silence had been his refuge for so long. It was hard to let go.

He turned to the fire, grasping hold of the mantel.

How could he tell her what he'd done? How would she trust him then?

But something inside Mitch told him that if he didn't try now, he never would. And a chance, infinitely precious, would be lost to him forever.

Perrie watched the struggle. Mitch was a very private man, never more alone than now.

''I killed my mother.'' His voice was harsh. Unyielding. Dark with pain.

She stemmed the shock of his words. ''I don't believe you.''

His dark head jerked up. Eyes that were black

holes of agony bored into her gaze. Silence spun out, then finally he spoke. "She was the gentlest person I ever knew. The mother every kid should have. Never too busy to read a story or bake cookies or hand out hugs." He looked straight at her. "She was a lot like you that way. Davey doesn't know how good he's got it."

Perrie held her breath, for fear of stemming the flow of this bounty of words from such a private man.

"When I was sixteen, I was a hell-raiser—full of myself, full of itches to be grown, to be gone, to live anywhere but Morning Star, Texas." He glanced away, unseeing. "I don't know why. My brother, Boone, was two years younger, and he loved the ranch. Couldn't get enough of any of it, especially horses. Me, I couldn't wait to get away. My dad and I locked horns almost every day."

More emotion than she'd ever seen swept across his face. Longing. Anguish. Anger.

"I came home drunk one night—one of many nights—and my dad and I got in a big fight. I threw some words around without caring where they hit. Told him I'd had it, I was moving out. He told me the sooner the better."

Sixteen. Still more boy than man, Perrie thought.

"I loaded up my stuff and left, a lot of harsh words between us. My mom was crying, and I remember hearing them fighting as I drove away."

Darkness shadowed his face. "The night was rainy, and I was drunk and mad and driving like a bat out of hell. I almost hit a truck, but he swerved and missed me. He lost control and hit a car down the road behind me.''

Then despair like she'd never seen washed over him. ''My mother had jumped in her car to come after me. It was her car that he hit.'' Mitch paused, as if he couldn't bear to continue.

Perrie clenched her hands, her palms wet. She wanted to stop him, to tell him he didn't have to say any more.

He swallowed hard. ''I saw the crash in my rear-view mirror. I turned around and went back. And found her.''

One hand covered her mouth. Perrie didn't want to hear any more, but he needed to tell her.

He lifted his gaze to hers, his dark eyes so filled with torment that Perrie wanted to cry out herself. She took a step toward him, but Mitch held up a hand to stop her.

''She died in my arms, but not before she told me not to let my anger win. She asked me to take care of Dad and Boone. Told me she—'' He swallowed hard. ''She loved me. I killed her because I couldn't control my hot head—and she's telling me how sorry she is for me. Telling me she loves me.''

Perrie couldn't stand back and let him suffer. Crossing to him, she grabbed his hand. ''It was an accident, Mitch. A terrible, tragic accident. You didn't mean it to happen.''

He jerked away and roared. ''Of course I didn't—but that didn't matter. She was still dead—

the best person I ever knew. And I was walking around without a scratch.'' He raked fingers through his hair. ''My dad never forgave me, and I can't blame him. He loved her with every breath in his body, and the last words they spoke were in anger—because of me. Because I couldn't control my goddamned feelings, couldn't see anyone outside myself.''

He straightened abruptly. Like some kind of robot had taken over, his features became hard as sheet metal. ''My father was so insane with grief that he tried to have me arrested for murder. The sheriff told him it was an accident, but my dad was right. I killed her, just like I'd taken out a gun and done it on purpose. He banned me from the funeral and told me he had only one son. Told me to get the hell out and never come back.''

Mitch turned to face her, his voice emotionless, though she could see, in his eyes, the wounded creature still writhing in pain. ''I never went back. And now it's too late.''

''Why?''

Though his voice was still impassive, she could see tiny cracks in his control. ''I got a letter today, too. From my brother, Boone. A private investigator tracked me down. Boone wants me to come home.''

His eyes were the saddest thing she'd ever seen. ''I can go home now because my father's dead.''

Oh, God. What a horrible tragedy, for all of them, Perrie thought. No wonder he held himself so much apart from others, never formed bonds of any kind.

With all he'd suffered, how could she bring down more on him by involving him in the tangled web of her own life?

"Will you go?" she asked. "To see your brother?"

The mask dissolved, just a little. She saw the longing in his gaze before he shook his head. "I don't know."

"Don't you miss him?"

"I don't know him anymore."

"I've seen you look at Davey. There's so much more to you than you admit, Mitch. You need a family. You need to let yourself be loved."

"You need to face Simon," he shot back. "Are you going to do it?"

Perrie recoiled, then stared at him, wondering how she'd been so wrong in the beginning. He wasn't cold and unfeeling as she'd assumed—if anything, Mitch felt too much. He'd lived for many years consumed by guilt and needless pain over what had basically been a youthful mistake, however tragic the consequences. His father had wronged him badly, but Mitch still heaped all the blame on himself, taking responsibility that wasn't all his.

Just like he'd taken her and Davey on, despite his preference to remain alone. Though she'd once seen only a loner and a drifter, the days had shown her a man capable of deep caring, a man who had been as good a father figure as she could ever have conjured up for her son. Who'd been kind to her even when he'd thought the worst of her. Who had shown her tantalizing glimpses of just how a woman could be cherished—until she'd forced him away.

What more could they have together if she would take a chance? If she would go back to Boston and end Simon's threat to their lives? She'd made a big mistake in judgment with Simon, but Mitch was Simon's polar opposite. He'd shown them in a thousand ways just how worthy he was of their trust.

She wanted more time with him, more space to let love grow. For she knew, deep in her heart, that love was what this was all about. A love deserving of a chance that she could provide—if she'd go back.

But she couldn't take Davey back there. Couldn't risk it. Then an idea popped into her head.

I wish you could be my dad, Mitch. She could hear Davey's words ringing in her head.

"Mitch?"

He turned from his contemplation of the fire.

"Do you want me?"

He looked stunned. "What the hell kind of question is that?"

"A simple question. With a simple answer."

He shook his head. "It's not simple at all."

"Then I've got my answer. No." Shoulders sagging, she turned away and started packing.

His big hand gripped her shoulder, spun her around. "Why are you asking me this?" His eyes shot fire at her, dark and edgy.

"Because I—" Nerves bolted up her spine, crushing her chest. Sucking in a deep breath, clasping her hands tightly together, she forced herself to go on. "I want you. I want you in my life, but I don't want you hurt by Simon. I want what Davey wants, but he's braver about asking."

His fingers dug into her arms. "Haven't you heard a word I've said? People who care about me die."

"One person," she whispered.

"What?" His eyes were wild now, like he wanted to be anyplace but here.

She swallowed. "One person died. And it was an accident."

His jaw tightened. "She's still dead. My family still disintegrated."

Perrie got mad then, and anger gave her courage. "That was your father's fault, not yours."

"Don't you understand? I don't know the first thing about love."

"You're so wrong. I've watched you with Davey." She glanced down, then forced her gaze back up. "I've felt your touch."

His eyes went black then, coals of memory smoldering. "That was only—"

She covered his mouth with her hand. "Don't you tell me that was only sex. I've had only sex.

This was different. We made love, Mitch. My heart and your heart—they touched.''

She felt her knees tremble as she waited for him to scoff.

But he didn't. Instead, sadness filled his gaze before he looked away. ''It doesn't matter.'' He shook his head. ''I can't be what you need. I don't know anything about families.''

''I think your mother would disagree.''

His head shot up, his eyes sparking with the merest glimpse of hope.

It was a start. Only time would convince him. Time they didn't have, unless she went back and faced Simon.

''I need your help, Mitch.''

''With what?''

''I want to leave Davey with you while I go back to Boston to testify.''

For the second time that day, Mitch looked stunned. ''Leave him with me?''

She rushed to explain. ''I know it's a lot of trouble, but I just can't risk having him in Boston until I know that Simon can't harm him. He would be so happy with you and—''

Mitch held up a hand. ''He's not a problem.'' Then he frowned. ''You would leave him with me, even after what I told you?''

''Of course I would.''

''You're going back?''

''You were right. It's what I have to do, or he

and I will never be free.'' She lifted her gaze to his. ''And there will never be a chance for us.''

When he started shaking his head slowly, her heart sank. She could see a war going on inside him as he stared into the fire.

Mitch heard her words, all of them, but believing them was something different. Yet, he saw the dream she offered. Deep within him, hope stirred.

Her courage shamed him. She was willing to face a man who terrified her—to give them a chance. He might have doubts the size of these mountains that they could make this work, but how could he do less?

He turned back to face her, seeing her pallor, the hands so tightly clasped.

He spoke up. ''I can't let you leave Davey here—''

Her shoulders sagged.

''But we'll go with you.''

Her eyes shot wide open.

''I don't just want Davey safe. I want you safe, too. I don't want you near Simon alone,'' Mitch said.

Joy flared in her eyes, then dimmed. ''But Davey—''

''I'll take care of Davey, don't you worry. But you're not going alone.''

''Mitch, I don't want you in Simon's path.''

He settled his hands on her shoulders, this time caressing. ''Honey, I'm not doubting you that he's dangerous, but I can take care of myself—and you and Davey. If you're going to face this, we're going to do it together.''

He stroked her cheek and drew her close. ''And when you're done, I have something to ask of you.''

Her lips parted, almost on a sigh. ''What is it?''

''You're right, too. I need to go back home. I want to see Boone and his new wife. But I want more than that.''

''What?''

He drew in a deep breath. ''I want you to go with me. I want to marry you. And whether or not I can ever adopt him, I want to be Davey's dad.''

She looked stunned now herself. ''Mitch, I—''

''I don't have a lot to offer you, Perrie, so you'd better think hard before you answer. This cabin and my truck are all I own in the world.''

''I've had luxury, Mitch. It's empty without love.''

Love. His heart leapt. ''I don't know how good I am at love. But what I have is yours…if you want it.''

He thought he saw tears glisten, but she didn't speak.

He rushed to bolster his argument. ''I've always worked hard, and I can do whatever it takes to make a life for us. I'll take good care of you both, I promise.''

Then he stopped, realizing just how much he wanted her to say yes. He dug deep. ''I don't want

to be alone anymore, Perrie. You and Davey—
you've made me want more.''

Her voice wasn't steady when she spoke. ''I
don't have much to offer, either.''

Mitch ducked his head, relief flooding through
him. Then he fixed his gaze on hers, pulling her
close. ''You have the world to offer. The biggest
heart that was ever packed into such a tiny frame.
And a lifetime of stories to make up for our children.'' Brushing his mouth across hers, he delighted
in how easily her lips parted for him. He stroked
his tongue over ruby satin.

''Children?'' she said weakly.

''I haven't had a family in a long time. I've got
a lot of ground to make up.'' His eyes studied hers.
''I don't know if I can be the right kind of father,
but I'll give it everything I've got.'' He kissed her
once more. ''You've brought me alive again. I'll
spend my life seeing that you never regret it.''

''Mitch, would you say—'' She worried at that
delectable lower lip, her lashes sweeping downward
as she shook her head.

Mitch frowned. ''What?''

''Never mind. I just wanted to hear—'' Her voice
trailed off as she toyed with a button on his shirt.

Then Perrie lifted her head, her expression res-
olute. ''No. I was weak before. I won't be weak
now. I'll say it first.''

Mitch wondered what she meant, but not for
long. Her hands slid up his chest, then framed his

face, her eyes so serious, yet so soft. So full. "I love you, Mitch."

He couldn't believe how it felt. How much he'd needed to hear those words, after being alone so long. He grasped her hands in his own much larger ones, bringing them down to his lips while he struggled to bring his voice under control.

"I—" Mitch swallowed hard, but the lump remained. "I've never told a woman this before, not since—" His chest felt too tight.

Gripping her hands between his, he pressed them to his heart. "I love you, Perrie. I'll protect you and honor you and do everything in my power to make you glad that you gave me your love."

Her eyes were so tender that he found himself unbearably moved. "I want your babies, Mitch. I want to make a family with you. A real family, filled with love."

For a moment, he couldn't speak. "Davey will always be our first child, but I'd like to give you others." Tenderly he kissed her, trying to tell her what she meant to him. All too soon the kiss turned hot.

She pressed her body along the length of his. "Mitch?"

He tried to listen over the sizzle of sparks shooting down his spine. "Yes?" He trailed kisses down her throat, loving the hitch in her breath. Then he sealed his mouth to hers again, tightening his fingers in her hair. He couldn't get close enough. He wanted to crawl inside her skin.

For endless moments, they lost themselves in the kiss and the promises it sealed. Finally he pulled away long enough to breathe.

"Mitch?" she said again, lake-blue eyes shining with something that looked almost like mischief.

"What?" He'd never get enough of looking at her. He'd dedicate his life to making her smile.

Then he learned where Davey had gotten that crafty expression as those lush lips curved, a glint in her eye. "Think we could start practicing tonight?"

Mitch laughed, and it felt like he'd been reborn. Love. Laughter. He wanted years of both.

He scooped her up in his arms, his spirits soaring. "Tonight. Forever. For as long as you like."

Epilogue

Morning Star, Texas

Boston—and Simon—were in her past now.

And Mitch was more than ready to be her future.

Perrie's hand gripped his as they turned up the road leading to the place that he'd once called home.

"Wow, Mitch, you lived up in that house on top of the hill? Are these your cows? Mom, look, there's a horse and another horse and a baby—"

Davey's excited chatter eased the ice that held Mitch's heart in its grip. Memories assaulted him from every direction.

Perrie answered. "Yes, sweetie. Boone lives there now, with his wife, Maddie."

"I wonder if he's big like Mitch."

I guess we'll find out, Perrie thought.

And then Mitch saw a man who had to be his brother, walking down the steps of the big white two-story house that had haunted Mitch's dreams. He stopped the car, and Perrie squeezed his hand.

"We'll just wait here."

Mitch jerked his gaze away from his brother's tall form, glancing at the woman who had changed his life. "No. You're my family now. You come with me."

With Perrie at his side and Davey holding his hand tightly, Mitch crossed the grass. His heart in his throat, he studied his brother.

The boy had grown into a man as tall as himself, the blond hair turned a darker gold. He had the look of their father, though Mitch had Sam's coloring. And in the blue eyes, Mitch saw the same swirl of emotion that crowded his own chest.

"Welcome home, Mitch," said a voice too deep to belong to his little brother. Boone broke away from the dark-haired beauty at his side and closed the distance between them.

Perrie watched the two big men clasp hands. Then Boone pulled Mitch into a hug that brought tears to her eyes. A few feet away, a statuesque gypsy with a mass of chestnut curls smiled and wept unashamedly as she winked at Perrie.

This must be Maddie. Perrie liked her on sight.

"Why's everybody crying, Mom?" Davey whispered.

"It's a good kind of crying, sweetheart."

Mitch stood at the window of Boone's office and looked out across land he'd never expected to lay eyes on again. "A sister—" He couldn't take it in. "Our mother and Maddie's father, before Mom married Dad?"

"Yeah." Boone clapped one hand to his shoulder. "You're taking the news better than I did. I couldn't believe Mom could ever give a child up, but she thought Dalton was dead, and back in those days—"

Mitch shook his head. "It had to just about kill her."

"I suspect it did." Boone cleared his throat. "I don't think Dad ever knew. But he found out later that Dalton was alive, and he never told Mom for fear she'd leave him. He gave Maddie this house because by rights, it should have been hers."

"Think Mom would have left Dad for Dalton if she'd known?"

Boone shook his head. "I don't think she ever would have left the two of us. And I think she honestly loved Dad." He exhaled sharply. "But I guess we'll never know."

Mitch thought of Perrie, of how she'd fought for her cub like a tigress, and suddenly he was sure.

"Mom would have stayed." He looked out the window again. "She'd be here still, if I hadn't—"

"That's over, Mitch. You can't blame yourself."

But he did and probably always would. Right now he had to set something else straight. "Boone, I—" After all he'd heard about what had happened after he was gone, he owed Boone a bigger apology than he'd ever dreamed. "I'm sorry. If I'd known what would happen to you after I left, I—"

"No apology needed. Dad should have handled all of it better, but Mom was everything to him. It drove him half out of his mind that their last words had been angry. He finally realized what he'd lost, but it was too late—for all of us."

"I can't believe he's gone. And I never got to—"

"Me, either. He was already dead before I knew. But he left something for you." Boone held out an envelope with Mitch's name scrawled in his father's bold hand.

Mitch eyed it warily.

Boone's mouth quirked. "I know. I didn't want to open mine, either. But it was all right." He paused. "Want me to leave you alone?"

Mitch shook his head. He'd been alone plenty long. He tore open the envelope and read.

Son—

I expect I lost the right to call you that a long time ago. It's the biggest regret of my life. I don't make any excuses for what I did—there aren't any excuses for it. I loved your mother so much that I just couldn't get past losing her, but in doing so, I lost two fine sons. I'd give everything I own to take it all back, but it's too late for any of that. I'm dying, and all I can hope is that you'll be found so that you'll finally know how sorry I am.

I hope you'll come home one day, to the place where you should have been all these years but for an old man's pride and stubborn blindness. I don't know what life has done to you since that terrible night, but I hope it's been better to you than I was.

Your mother wouldn't be proud of me. All Jenny ever wanted in life was to make the people she loved happy, and she did that for all of us, every day of her short life. I think they broke the mold when they made her, but if there are two women out there with hearts as big as hers, I hope you and Boone find them and get back some of what you lost.

It was an accident, Mitch. You never would have hurt her on purpose. She would tell you to let it go. She loved you with every breath in her body. It was just one of those terrible trials that life hands us. Some of us handle them right, and some of us fail.

I failed you, son. If it's any consolation, I've paid every day since. I wronged you, and it's

my everlasting regret that I won't live long
enough to tell you in person. I don't expect
you to forgive me, but I do hope someday
you'll have a son of your own and you can do
right everything that I did so very wrong.

Dad

"Mitch?"

At the sound of Perrie's voice, Mitch turned from
the window. He didn't know how long he'd been
staring off into the distance. He held out his arms
and she came into them without hesitation.

"Davey's asleep. Are you all right?"

He handed her the letter and met his brother's
gaze over her head while she read it. Boone's eyes
said that he understood. All Mitch could do was
shake his head. So much loss. So much pain.

Perrie's golden head lifted, her blue eyes swimming with tears. She glanced back at Boone, then
over at Maddie who'd entered the room, silvery
eyes sympathetic. She turned again to Mitch. "That
poor man." She sighed. "I wanted to hate him for
what he did to you, but now I just feel sad for him."

Maddie spoke up then, snuggling against Boone
as he pulled her close. "I never knew Jenny, but I
feel like I did. I think I know what she'd say." She
looked around the room at each of them. "I think
she'd say that love was the legacy she wanted to
leave, however short or long her life was."

She would tell you to let it go. Mitch knew his father had been right—it was time to move on.

Mitch felt his throat tighten, saw a sheen in Boone's eyes. "Love was everything to her. She handed it out like it was water, free and easy to find. Like a spring that would replenish itself, the more she gave away." He held on to Perrie tightly. "But it takes some of us longer than others to believe that."

His brother nodded, then looked down at Maddie, love arcing between the two of them, so bright it filled the room.

Mitch looked at Perrie. "I don't know where we'll wind up, but I know I'd like for us to start here. What would you think about getting married in Morning Star?"

Tears trembled on her lashes as she smiled. "I think it would be perfect. Here, with the people Jenny loved so very much."

"Except one," Maddie reminded.

"But we'll find her," Boone insisted.

Around the room, heads nodded solemnly and silent promises were exchanged.

Maddie said it for all of them. "And then we'll bring her home to Morning Star."

Home, Mitch thought. Wherever Perrie was would be his home now. Morning Star was just a place.

But it was a special place, finally free of ghosts, a place where he could always return. Here, where he'd first learned about love, he now felt the blessing of forgiveness, the return of bright memory instead of dark, angry pain.

It was fitting that here he would bind to him the woman who had given him love when he'd thought himself forever alone. In this place where he'd once lost all hope of love, he would begin again. He would speak vows that he would never break: to love, honor and cherish, to guard this woman and her children with his life.

Finally Mitch felt free, felt the darkness, so long his companion, slip away. "I love you, Perrie," he whispered into her honey-gold hair.

"I love you, Mitch." Her arms stole around his waist, clasping him tightly. "Welcome home."

He was home at last. Home in the arms of love.

* * * * *

Be sure to look for the emotional story of Boone and Mitch's long-lost sister. Coming soon from Jean Brashear, only in Silhouette Special Edition.

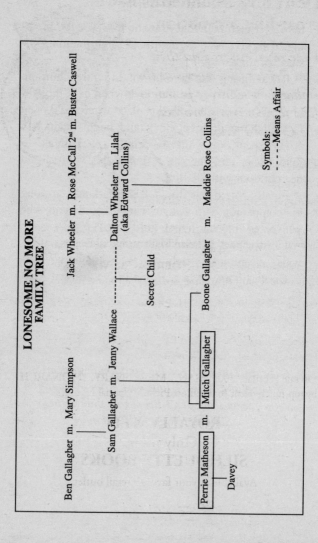

LONESOME NO MORE
FAMILY TREE

Ben Gallagher m. Mary Simpson

Jack Wheeler m. Rose McCall 2ⁿᵈ m. Buster Caswell

Sam Gallagher m. Jenny Wallace ----- Dalton Wheeler m. Lilah
(aka Edward Collins)

Secret Child

Mitch Gallagher   Boone Gallagher   m.   Maddie Rose Collins

Perrie Matheson

Davey

Symbols:
- - - - Means Affair

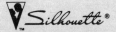

If you enjoyed what you just read,
then we've got an offer you can't resist!

Take 2 bestselling love stories FREE!

Plus get a FREE surprise gift!

PAMELA TOTH
DIANA WHITNEY
ALLISON LEIGH
LAURIE PAIGE
bring you four heartwarming stories
in the brand-new series

So Many Babies

At the Buttonwood Baby Clinic,
babies and romance abound!

On sale January 2000: **THE BABY LEGACY**
by Pamela Toth

On sale February 2000: **WHO'S THAT BABY?**
by Diana Whitney

On sale March 2000: **MILLIONAIRE'S INSTANT BABY**
by Allison Leigh

On sale April 2000: **MAKE WAY FOR BABIES!**
by Laurie Paige

Only from Silhouette SPECIAL EDITION
Available at your favorite retail outlet.

Silhouette ®
Where love comes alive™

Visit us at www.romance.net   SSESMB

MONTANA MAVERICKS
Big Sky Brides

Legendary love comes to Whitehorn, Montana,
once more as beloved authors

Christine Rimmer, Jennifer Greene and Cheryl St.John

present three brand-new stories in this exciting anthology!

Meet the Brennan women:
SUZANNA, DIANA and ISABELLE

Strong-willed beauties who find unexpected
love in these irresistible marriage of
covnenience stories.

Don't miss
MONTANA MAVERICKS: BIG SKY BRIDES
On sale in February 2000,
only from Silhouette Books!

Available at your favorite retail outlet.

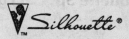

Silhouette®

Visit us at www.romance.net

PSMMBSB

Back by popular demand!

CHRISTINE RIMMER
SUSAN MALLERY
CHRISTINE FLYNN

prescribe three more exciting doses of heart-stopping romance in their series, **PRESCRIPTION: MARRIAGE.**

Three wedding-shy female physicians discover that marriage may be just what the doctor ordered when they lose their hearts to three irresistible, iron-willed men.

Look for this wonderful series at your favorite retail outlet—

On sale December 1999:
A DOCTOR'S VOW (SE #1293)
by **Christine Rimmer**

On sale January 2000:
THEIR LITTLE PRINCESS (SE #1298)
by **Susan Mallery**

On sale February 2000:
DR. MOM AND THE MILLIONAIRE (SE #1304)
by **Christine Flynn**

Only from
Silhouette Special Edition

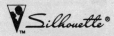

Visit us at www.romance.net

SILHOUETTE'S 20ᵀᴴ ANNIVERSARY CONTEST
OFFICIAL RULES
NO PURCHASE NECESSARY TO ENTER

1. To enter, follow directions published in the offer to which you are responding. Contest begins 1/1/00 and ends on 8/24/00 (the "Promotion Period"). Method of entry may vary. Mailed entries must be postmarked by 8/24/00, and received by 8/31/00.

2. During the Promotion Period, the Contest may be presented via the Internet. Entry via the Internet may be restricted to residents of certain geographic areas that are disclosed on the Web site. To enter via the Internet, if you are a resident of a geographic area in which Internet entry is permissible, follow the directions displayed on-line, including typing your essay of 100 words or fewer telling us "Where In The World Your Love Will Come Alive." On-line entries must be received by 11:59 p.m. Eastern Standard time on 8/24/00. Limit one e-mail entry per person, household and e-mail address per day, per presentation. If you are a resident of a geographic area in which entry via the Internet is permissible, you may, in lieu of submitting an entry on-line, enter by mail, by hand-printing your name, address, telephone number and contest number/name on an 8"x 11" plain piece of paper and telling us in 100 words or fewer "Where In The World Your Love Will Come Alive," and mailing via first-class mail to: Silhouette 20ᵗʰ Anniversary Contest, (in the U.S.) P.O. Box 9069, Buffalo, NY 14269-9069; (In Canada) P.O. Box 637, Fort Erie, Ontario, Canada L2A 5X3. Limit one 8"x 11" mailed entry per person, household and e-mail address per day. On-line and/or 8"x 11" mailed entries received from persons residing in geographic areas in which Internet entry is not permissible will be disqualified. No liability is assumed for lost, late, incomplete, inaccurate, nondelivered or misdirected mail, or misdirected e-mail, for technical, hardware or software failures of any kind, lost or unavailable network connection, or failed, incomplete, garbled or delayed computer transmission or any human error which may occur in the receipt or processing of the entries in the contest.

3. Essays will be judged by a panel of members of the Silhouette editorial and marketing staff based on the following criteria:

   Sincerity (believability, credibility)—50%

   Originality (freshness, creativity)—30%

   Aptness (appropriateness to contest ideas)—20%

   Purchase or acceptance of a product offer does not improve your chances of winning. In the event of a tie, duplicate prizes will be awarded.

4. All entries become the property of Harlequin Enterprises Ltd., and will not be returned. Winner will be determined no later than 10/31/00 and will be notified by mail. Grand Prize winner will be required to sign and return Affidavit of Eligibility within 15 days of receipt of notification. Noncompliance within the time period may result in disqualification and an alternative winner may be selected. All municipal, provincial, federal, state and local laws and regulations apply. Contest open only to residents of the U.S. and Canada who are 18 years of age or older, and is void wherever prohibited by law. Internet entry is restricted solely to residents of those geographical areas in which Internet entry is permissible. Employees of Torstar Corp., their affiliates, agents and members of their immediate families are not eligible. Taxes on the prizes are the sole responsibility of winners. Entry and acceptance of any prize offered constitutes permission to use winner's name, photograph or other likeness for the purposes of advertising, trade and promotion on behalf of Torstar Corp. without further compensation to the winner, unless prohibited by law. Torstar Corp and D.L. Blair, Inc., their parents, affiliates and subsidiaries, are not responsible for errors in printing or electronic presentation of contest or entries. In the event of printing or other errors which may result in unintended prize values or duplication of prizes, all affected contest materials or entries shall be null and void. If for any reason the Internet portion of the contest is not capable of running as planned, including infection by computer virus, bugs, tampering, unauthorized intervention, fraud, technical failures, or any other causes beyond the control of Torstar Corp. which corrupt or affect the administration, secrecy, fairness, integrity or proper conduct of the contest, Torstar Corp. reserves the right, at its sole discretion, to disqualify any individual who tampers with the entry process and to cancel, terminate, modify or suspend the contest or the Internet portion thereof. In the event of a dispute regarding an on-line entry, the entry will be deemed submitted by the authorized holder of the e-mail account submitted at the time of entry. Authorized account holder is defined as the natural person who is assigned to an e-mail address by an Internet access provider, on-line service provider or other organization that is responsible for arranging e-mail address for the domain associated with the submitted e-mail address.

5. Prizes: Grand Prize—a $10,000 vacation to anywhere in the world. Travelers (at least one must be 18 years of age or older) or parent or guardian if one traveler is a minor, must sign and return a Release of Liability prior to departure. Travel must be completed by December 31, 2001, and is subject to space and accommodations availability. Two hundred (200) Second Prizes—a two-book limited edition autographed collector set from one of the Silhouette Anniversary authors: Nora Roberts, Diana Palmer, Linda Howard or Annette Broadrick (value $10.00 each set). All prizes are valued in U.S. dollars.

6. For a list of winners (available after 10/31/00), send a self-addressed, stamped envelope to: Harlequin Silhouette 20ᵗʰ Anniversary Winners, P.O. Box 4200, Blair, NE 68009-4200.

Contest sponsored by Torstar Corp., P.O. Box 9042, Buffalo, NY 14269-9042.

PS20RULES

**ENTER FOR
A CHANCE TO WIN***

Silhouette's 20ᵗʰ Anniversary Contest

Tell Us Where in the World
You Would Like *Your* Love To Come Alive...
And We'll Send the Lucky Winner There!

Silhouette wants to take you wherever
your happy ending can come true.

Here's how to enter: Tell us, in 100 words or less,
where you want to go to make your love come alive!

In addition to the grand prize, there will be 200
runner-up prizes, collector's-edition book sets
autographed by one of the Silhouette anniversary
authors: **Nora Roberts, Diana Palmer,
Linda Howard** or **Annette Broadrick**.

DON'T MISS YOUR CHANCE TO WIN!
ENTER NOW! No Purchase Necessary

Where love comes alive™

Name: _____

Address: _____

City: _____ State/Province: _____

Zip/Postal Code: _____

Mail to Harlequin Books: **In the U.S.**: P.O. Box 9069, Buffalo, NY
14269-9069; **In Canada**: P.O. Box 637, Fort Erie, Ontario, L4A 5X3

COMING NEXT MONTH

#1303 MAN...MERCENARY...MONARCH—Joan Elliott Pickart
Royally Wed

In the blink of an eye, John Colton discovered he was a Crown Prince, a brand-new father...and a man on the verge of falling for a woman in *his* royal family's employ. Yet trust—and love—didn't come easily to this one-time mercenary who desperately wanted to be son, brother, father...*husband?*

#1304 DR. MOM AND THE MILLIONAIRE—Christine Flynn
Prescription: Marriage

No woman had been able to get the powerful Chase Harrington anywhere near an altar. Then again, this confirmed bachelor had never met someone like the charmingly fascinating Dr. Alexandra Larson, a woman whose tender loving care promised to heal him, body, heart...and soul.

#1305 WHO'S THAT BABY?—Diana Whitney
So Many Babies

Johnny Winterhawk did what any red-blooded male would when he found a baby on his doorstep—he panicked. Pediatrician Claire Davis rescued him by offering her hand in a marriage of convenience...and then showed him just how real a family they could be.

#1306 CATTLEMAN'S COURTSHIP—Lois Faye Dyer

Experience made Quinn Bowdrie a tough man of the land who didn't need anybody. That is, until he met the sweetly tempting Victoria Denning, the only woman who could teach this stubborn rancher the pleasures of courtship.

#1307 THE MARRIAGE BASKET—Sharon De Vita
The Blackwell Brothers

Rina Roberts had her heart set on adopting her orphaned nephew. But the boy's godfather, Hunter Blackwell, stood in her way. Their love for the child drew them together and Rina knew that not only did the handsome doctor hold the key to Billy's future—but also to her own heart.

#1308 FALLING FOR AN OLDER MAN—Trisha Alexander
Callahans & Kin

Sheila Callahan dreamed of picket fences and wedding rings, but Jack Kinsella, the man of her dreams, wasn't the slightest bit interested in commitment, especially not to his best friend's younger sister. But one night together created more than just passion....